EMILY REFERMAT

THE INVISIBLE WAR

Black Rose Writing | Texas

ISBN: 978-1-68513-434-1
PUBLISHED BY BLACK ROSE WRITING
www.blackrosewriting.com

Printed in the United States of America
Suggested Retail Price (SRP) $21.95

The Invisible War is printed in Garamond Premier Pro

Dedicated to Joe and Tina for your ever-enduring support.

THE INVISIBLE WAR

CHAPTER 1

Garrison crossed his arms. His mother kept glancing at him from the driver's seat, but he was choosing to ignore her.

"You know," she began, "I used to really enjoy going to the farm."

Garrison didn't respond.

"I know you're unhappy and I'm sorry plans changed."

Garrison shook his head. It was too much. "Dad said I could come for the summer! To his new apartment where he has an 8K High Definition TV. 8K, Mom! Do you even know what that means?"

"You don't need more TV. You need to connect with people." She looked at him. "Think of this trip as a real-life video game where you're the star."

Garrison rolled his eyes. "Hero, Mom. Not star. And how am I supposed to do that in the middle of nowhere?" He sighed. "I can't believe Dad bailed again. He never keeps his word. It's like he doesn't even want to be around me."

"Mmm."

The guilt got him before he was prepared for it. It ate at his insides like radioactive moths feasting on a wool sweater. He watched her force a smile, which just made it worse.

"The farm is surrounded by miles of woods. When I was your age, I explored them every summer. I dug hideouts; hid treasures. Think of how much fun you could have."

"Fun. Right. You know, I heard what she said. Your phone was on speaker. She doesn't even want me to come."

He thought back to the conversation a few days before. He had walked into the kitchen for dinner when he heard his grandmother's voice. An odd event, considering it wasn't a holiday. She asked about his mother's upcoming trip.

His mother paused while straining the spaghetti and turned to her phone on the counter. "About that. Actually, Gary has a new merger he has to negotiate, so he can't take Garrison anymore."

"Figures."

His mother dumped the pasta in the strainer with a loud plop. "Yeah. So...I'm wondering if you could watch Garrison this summer."

"Oh!" There was a pause. "Sorry, Rachel, but I can't leave. Someone needs to feed and water the hens. Plus, there's the weeding and planting."

"No. No. I mean, can Garrison come stay with you?"

"Here?!" The word was too loud, almost panicky.

The microwave beeped. "Yes, there," said his mother, clearly frustrated. She went over, opened the microwave door, and grabbed the jar of pasta sauce. "Ouch."

"What happened?"

"Nothing. A hot jar." His mother stuck her fingers in her mouth. "I really need your help."

"What about his other grandparents?"

"Really, Mom? Anyway, they're on a three-week cruise and won't be back until July."

His grandmother stammered a little, then talked very fast. "I'd love to help, but the house isn't really set up for children."

His mother wasn't giving up. "He's 14. It's not like you have to babysit him. He won't be any trouble. Most of the time, he even makes his own meals."

His grandmother made some strange sounds on the other side, like whooshing air. "The chickens are sick," she finally blurted. "What if it's contagious?"

His mother rolled her eyes. "It's not the avian flu, Mom. It'll be fine."

"But—"

His mother didn't let her finish. "Seriously, Mom. What is wrong? I ask for help this one time and you make excuses. You never invite us over. You've barely seen him over the years. Don't you want to get to know your ONLY grandson?"

"Of course."

"Then do this for me. Doctors without Borders is my dream."

There was silence.

His mother pushed the advantage. "Think of this as a way to get to know Garrison better. Who knows? Maybe you'll find you have things in common."

His grandmother sighed loudly. "Fine."

The irritation and displeasure in that final word haunted him, even now, in the car on the way to her house.

"Your grandmother wants you to come," his mother said, staring at the road ahead. He got the feeling she was avoiding eye contact. "She's just...busy. It's the stress. She's been handling the farm on her own since my father, your grandfather, died years ago. She just doesn't realize how she comes across."

Garrison didn't believe that, but wasn't going to argue. He changed tack. "Why can't you just not go?"

"I made a commitment."

"So?"

"A commitment is a promise and I don't break my promises."

Garrison sighed. He knew she was thinking of his father, in Chicago at this very moment, brokering another sales deal for people who already had too much money.

"Besides, it's only for a few weeks," she said. "I'll be back before you know it."

Garrison raised an eyebrow. "In that case, why not just leave me home by myself?"

She made a face. "Because you're 14, not 18. That would be irresponsible."

"Yeah, and a few weeks actually means most of the summer."

His mother didn't reply.

Garrison glared out the window. There was nothing but fields edged with narrow strips of wild-looking trees. Not a skate park, video game store, or sign of civilization in sight.

He leaned back against the seat, turning his body away from his mother, and trying to ignore the pain that continued in his stomach.

A half hour after passing through a small town and another stretch of farm country, Garrison's mother finally pulled off into a gravel driveway. A giant maple tree with a tire swing stood on one side with a rusty wheel against a picket fence on the other. The sign said Wagon Wheel Farm.

It wasn't much of a farm, Garrison thought. Most of the property was taken up by the house. It was a massive white building with enough curly edges and layers of wood to look like a dollhouse, albeit one that needed repainting. In many places, the white was chipping.

"I have never understood why she puts out so many chairs," his mother said as she slowed down. "It would look so much better if it weren't so cluttered."

Garrison followed her gaze. On the large front porch, there were a lot of chairs — rocking chairs, folding chairs, chairs with big weaved backs that looked like thrones. Most of them were filled, the people watching their car.

His mother drove past them without a second glance, stopping on the side of the house several feet from a large red barn.

As Garrison got out of the car, his nose began to itch. Cut grass, hot dirt, and something like day-old dumpster were playing pinball in his nostrils. He glanced back at the porch. Some of the people came around the corner to watch them. Their expressions were not welcoming.

"Here he is," sang his mother.

Garrison noted the use of her fake cheery voice. He turned and saw his grandmother. She stood a few inches from his mom. They shared a family resemblance — same nose and eyebrow ridge. A face free of any makeup. However, where his mother had brown hair and brown eyes, Mae's were both gray and her hair was pulled back. She wore a collared pale purple shirt under a tan vest that was full of pockets. Her tan pants were tucked into black, plastic-looking boots. Overall, she somewhat resembled an old-fashioned explorer, especially next to his mom's t-shirt and jeans.

No one moved. No one hugged.

"Well..." said his mother after the silence stretched on, "I've gotta get going. I have the three-hour drive back and preparations still to finish. I appreciate this, Mom. I'll call when I get there, but I'm not sure what to expect after I'm at the hospital. Email is probably better."

His grandmother nodded.

"Garrison."

He turned to his mother.

"I want you to behave. Be p-o-l-i-t-e." She dragged out the word. "I'll miss you."

He looked into her face, one final plea to change her mind. She opened her arms. After only a slight hesitation, he went into them.

"I'll make it up to you," she whispered into his ear, "I promise. I love you." She squeezed tight. "Text me when you get settled."

Garrison's eyes were stinging, so he shut them and thought about something else.

Too quickly, his mother was in the car again and the dust from the rear wheels spat back at him.

He gave his grandmother a sidelong glance. "So what now...ah...Grandma?" He choked on the unfamiliar word.

She grimaced. "Just call me Mae," she said, turning towards the house. He really didn't know whether to feel surprised or relieved.

She led him through the side door, not towards the front porch, which he was thankful for, since all the people were still staring. They walked into a gigantic kitchen the color of vanilla ice cream. There were cabinets everywhere and two telephones attached to the wall. One plastic and one even older, metal, with a rotary dial. A couple people were standing near a large concrete topped island in the center.

"That him?" asked the boy. He was probably a little older than Garrison and dressed in a tight fitting black suit. Garrison felt the boy's eyes and tried to stand up straighter.

Mae didn't turn when she answered, "Mm. I'll put you in the front room."

"But that's my room," cried the boy.

The older man next to him shushed him. He was in a tanish vest and plaid pants.

"I'll do some rearranging," Mae said, then she stopped and turned towards Garrison. "Sorry. That was just me thinking aloud."

Garrison didn't know what to say to that, so he said nothing.

Mae frowned. "Now. Here are the rules. No going outside, no opening doors that are already closed. And no going upstairs. Actually, you know what, just stay in your room. I'll bring you your meals."

"Wait...what?"

Mae ignored him. "Yes. That's good," she muttered to herself before turning and walking out.

Garrison glanced at the others in the kitchen, trying to read their expressions. Was this normal?

The older man didn't react, but the boy brought his finger up to the side of his head and circled it there. *Crazy.*

Garrison didn't smile, but he felt a little better. He went after Mae. "So I'm a prisoner here?"

"No. You're a guest. And guests stay in their rooms."

Garrison didn't know what to say to that either.

They passed a narrow set of stairs off the kitchen, then went through a doorway into a large hall. The same cream color from the kitchen was on the walls and chunky woodwork along the ceiling. The hallway stretched out in front of him. It seemed almost impossibly long. They passed door after door after door, all of them closed. "Are all these guest rooms?" Garrison asked, losing count.

"A couple. Most are upstairs."

Garrison pondered that. They passed a grand two-story staircase with a chandelier, and the house just kept going.

"How many people are staying here?"

Mae stopped. "A dozen or so, but you won't meet them."

"I won't?"

Mae shook her head. "They won't be staying long. It's just me, usually."

Garrison recalled the people he saw on the porch. He was about to ask about them, but Mae opened one of the closed doors and pulled out two white towels and a washcloth. She thrust them into his arms and walked on. A few more doors and she stopped. She pulled a key ring from one of her vest pockets, flipping through a dozen old-fashioned keys. Finding the one she wanted, she thrust it into the lock, but didn't open the door. Garrison looked around. They walked almost the entire length of the house and were near the front door now.

"Your mother really didn't give me much notice," Mae said, drawing his attention back. She seemed to be closely examining the doorknob — clear glass cut to look like a large diamond. She rubbed at a spot. "It's not like I keep a spare room just in case. I haven't seen you in years."

Garrison glanced down. The moths were eating his stomach again. Mae muttered something he didn't quite catch and opened the door. Garrison followed her in and nearly dropped the towels.

The room was a horrible pale pink! It made him think of old ladies with knitting needles. What was it called? Mauve!

What wasn't painted mauve, covered in mauve upholstery or white with mauve flowers on it, was covered in lace. It trimmed the dual twin bed quilts, covered the two side tables and perched on twin chairs like floppy snowflakes.

Garrison closed his eyes. This couldn't be real.

He opened them again.

The room was still there, still mauve, still awful. He barely noticed when Mae left, quietly closing the door behind her.

CHAPTER 2

"Fart nuggets!" Garrison threw down his portable video game after dying for a fifth time. Though it was a sorry-I'm-too-busy-for-you present from his father, it helped take his mind off his current situation. But now he was frustrated. He looked around. There were two beds in the room and two dressers. At first, he was worried about sharing. After all, that boy in the kitchen called this his room. Although, for the life of him, Garrison could not understand why anyone would want such a place. A few hours passed, however, and no one showed up to claim the space. Garrison supposed that meant it was his. At least there was an attached bathroom. That was convenient. Plus, it was blessedly white tile. No pink in sight.

Garrison took his cell phone from his pocket. It was from his mom, so nothing fancy — prepaid Android. She said it was more than enough. He should be grateful. Yet, there was no service.

He went into settings to search for Wi-Fi. Not a single modem appeared. He wondered how that was even possible. Unsure what to do next, he leaned back against the bed pillows. The ceiling had cracks running all through it. And the plaster was uneven in places, making ridges and valleys. If he squinted, it almost looked like a 3-D map. He imagined deltas and mountain ranges. Then something registered in his brain. Someone was yelling. Garrison could tell it was a man, or maybe a couple of men, near the front of the house. He got up and opened his bedroom door.

Through the front windows, he could see the people on the porch bunched up into a group. A word rose above the din. "Thief!"

Curious, Garrison decided to move closer. No one else was in the hall. Just as he reached the door, a deep voice said, "I planned to turn it in."

Garrison looked through the door's intricate main window. In the middle of the group of people on the porch was the boy from the kitchen. He was glaring at a man in a brown suit, who was, for some reason, sucking on his fingers.

"Of course you did," said the boy. "Hence, it's in your pocket."

The brown suited man bent over him menacingly. "Are you accusing me of something, Tuck?"

The boy didn't seem intimidated. He crossed his arms. "I believe that's exactly what I'm doing."

Garrison saw this type of standoff after school sometimes, behind the maintenance shed. He held his breath.

Suddenly, Mae came up the porch stairs. Her boots echoed on the wood, making everyone turn. They all started talking at once. "Enough," she shouted. "We have plenty of problems without accusations being bandied about." She looked at the boy. "People are innocent until proven guilty." She didn't wait for a response, but turned to the front door.

Garrison stared, mesmerized by the aura of power that surrounded her. He never saw that before. People moved out of her way. They looked down as her gaze settled on them. It was unnerving. He didn't want to be next. He stepped back from the door, searching for a place to hide. There was a large grandfather clock nearby. He flattened himself against its side just as the door opened. He held his breath. Footsteps and Mae's back. She didn't stop.

When the hallway was quiet again, Garrison peeked out. On the porch, the tension was gone. People were back in chairs or leaning against the railings. Garrison stepped slowly through the door and looked around. The boy he saw in the kitchen earlier was still there. Tuck was what the big man called him. Garrison took a few steps in his direction.

Tuck met his eyes. "It took me weeks to perfect a shocking wallet," he said.

Garrison knew his mouth was open. "Was it his wallet?"

"No," answered a stocky blond man as he came towards them. He stopped, looking Garrison up and down for a moment. It felt a bit too long. Then the man smiled at Tuck, who stood up straighter.

"So young, yet so gifted. Whoever has been taking things will think twice now, all because of Tuck, here." The man clapped Tuck's shoulder.

Tuck nodded. "It was getting out of hand. People didn't feel safe. Someone had to do something."

"And you were perfect for the job," the blond man said. Then he winked at Garrison before going inside.

Garrison examined Tuck. Now that he was closer, he could see that Tuck's hair was short and black, spiked up a little. From the set of his eyes and round face, Garrison thought he could have Asian ancestry.

"You're Mae's grandson."

Garrison couldn't tell if it was a question or a statement, so he just nodded.

"Why are you here?"

Garrison was caught off guard at the accusatory tone. "What do you mean?"

Tuck raised an eyebrow. "Mae never mentioned you. EVER. And suddenly, now," he waved a hand out at the yard, "when all this is going on, you show up."

Garrison glanced quickly out, but saw only grass and farm buildings. He turned back. "You mean the stealing? I just got here today. It can't have anything to do with me."

Tuck leaned back a little. Garrison got the feeling he said something wrong. He decided he didn't want to talk anymore. He wasn't very good at this sort of thing, anyway. He retreated to his bedroom and shut the door. Grabbing the portable video game, his final thought was that dying a sixth time would be better than another embarrassing moment with people.

CHAPTER 3

A sharp rap sounded on Garrison's bedroom door the next morning. He stared at it through half-closed eyes.

There was more knocking.

He looked at the clock. 7AM. Who was up at this hour? He pushed the sheet aside and got out of bed. He half dragged himself to the door and opened it. Mae was on the other side.

"Um...hi." He noticed she didn't have a tray in her hand. It was strange since just yesterday, she brought him lunch and dinner. "Is breakfast not a meal I eat in my room?"

"No, and yes. It's likely you'll be joining us in the dining room from now on."

"Why?"

Mae looked away. "Because circumstances changed. Now come on."

"But...wait...I've got to get dressed." He suddenly realized he was standing there in his boxers. The door blocked his body, but he still moved further back behind it. "I'll need a minute."

Mae sighed. "Fine. Meet me in the kitchen when you're finally ready." She turned and left.

Garrison closed the door. He debated going back to bed, but his stomach growled. Mae also made him nervous. So, instead, he pulled on some clothes and left his room.

Just as he neared the kitchen door, Garrison heard voices. A man asked, "So, have you decided what to do with Tuck's revelation?"

Mae answered. "Act like things are normal. It's not like anyone is here to tell him differently."

Garrison wondered if they were talking about him. His mother would tell him they weren't. That eavesdroppers always believe what's being said is about them, because eavesdropping is wrong. Garrison rounded the kitchen door, hoping to see the man, but he only caught a glimpse of someone leaving.

"Syrup, butter, and strawberries are in the dining room," Mae said, handing him a plate of pancakes. She jerked her head towards a doorway to the left, then picked up a spatula and started another pancake. He looked at the food. He wanted to ask her about Tuck's revelation. About who wouldn't know it wasn't normal? But she might tell him to mind his own business. She might snap at him for being nosy and not belonging here. He decided to ignore it. She was probably talking about someone else, someone here, like the shocking wallet guy.

He walked through the doorway, passed through a small pantry, and then entered a huge room with two long rectangular tables. There were already 10 or so people sitting down and eating. It reminded him of a cafeteria, but in a really old house. Was his grandmother running a boarding house? Or maybe an inn?

He sat at the very end of one of the tables, avoiding eye contact with everyone. It wasn't hard. They gave him plenty of space, although he saw them glance his way now and then. Watching them, he felt strange. There was a buzzing in his head, but it wasn't a sound. This was something he experienced before. A name floated to the top of his mind. Arthur. His old imaginary friend. His stomach spasmed, making him gasp. He pushed the buzzing away, concentrating on the knot in his stomach. He must be hungry.

When Mae came in, she sat down across from him. "So," she said after several minutes. "What are your plans for the day?"

Garrison shrugged. "I guess go back to my room. And stay there. Forever."

She took a sip of coffee, staring at him. She swallowed loudly. "About that. I thought it over and you don't have to stay in your room all the time. Meals are in here at 7 for breakfast, noon, and then dinner at 6. You can explore a bit, but I have people staying here and I don't want you walking in on them, so still no opening closed doors. Okay?"

"Okay," is what he said. But he was thinking, WHAT?! Where is this coming from?

She took another sip of coffee. "If you want to go outside, you need to stay on the property. Where there's grass."

"What about the woods? You let my mom go in there."

Mae was shaking her head before he finished. "No. It's too dangerous. I mean it. Don't go out of bounds. You need to stay on the property."

Garrison finished eating, more confused than ever about his grandmother. Finally, he put his dishes in the tub he saw a few other people use. On the way back to his room, he heard whispering. He stopped to listen.

"It HAS to be that rebel group from a few years ago," said a woman. Her words came fast and breathy.

"Makes sense," replied another. "Although why change the name to CS?"

"Exactly," said a man. "What is happening now; it's not them. The rebels undermined the regime, played politics. This is different. Darker. And using each village as a battleground is just—" He stopped mid sentence as the trio rounded the corner and spotted Garrison. He dropped his gaze to the floor, but not before he saw all three of their eyes narrow in suspicion. They hurried past, giving him more than enough room.

Garrison tried to shake it off, although his stomach did an uncomfortable flip. He must have eaten too many pancakes. He hurried down the hall and found Tuck at his bedroom door.

"Want to come help me put red dye tablets in the upstairs taps?"

Garrison was puzzled for a moment, and then his brain supplied an image. You turn on the tap and red runs across your fingers, like blood. He almost laughed aloud. Then he thought of Mae and her rules. He shook his head. "I'm good." Although he couldn't help being a little jealous that Tuck was able to go upstairs.

Tuck's jaw tightened. "What? I'm not good enough for you?"

"That's not it. I..." Garrison couldn't say it. He couldn't tell another boy that he was scared of his grandmother. "I just want to play my video game."

Tuck took a moment to respond. "All day?"

"Well...um, yeah."

Tuck shook his head. "I can't believe I told Mae you seemed cool. Asked her if we could hang out." He marched off.

Garrison watched him go. Usually people didn't want to hang out with him. Had Tuck really told Mae he seemed cool? It was just like him to ruin everything. He pushed into his room, trying to shove away his feelings. He didn't want to be here. He didn't want to talk to anyone. He didn't want a friend or a grandmother or a delicious breakfast. He just wanted to go home.

He wasn't sure how long passed while he played his video game, maybe minutes, maybe hours. The level he was currently playing was very dark, the silhouette of trees menacing against a deep purple sky. The boss moved, sometimes on four legs, sometimes on two. The huge black crown on his head was impossibly tall. It glinted as he put his head down and charged Garrison's avatar. Garrison barely moved in time to avoid being skewered. He was low on health. The boss did something, and time seemed to stand still. Garrison couldn't move. But the boss could. One step at a time, closer and closer, getting taller and taller, until — KNOCK, KNOCK!

Garrison jumped in real life. He looked down at his controller, but the screen was black. He put it on the side table and went to open the door.

There was no one there. For a moment, Garrison wondered if the house was haunted. More likely, Tuck was playing ding, dong, ditch. Garrison looked at the clock — 11:52. That was close enough to get some lunch. He headed down the hall.

No one was in the kitchen, so Garrison ventured into the dining room. Trays of cold sandwiches and fruit salad were laid out on the side table. Garrison helped himself. He would take his food back to his room and eat while he leveled up.

***

Garrison was in the middle of a complicated run/jump sequence when he registered a smell. Well, several smells, really. Sauteing onions, melted butter, a sweet/savory mix he couldn't place, but made his mouth water. Was it dinnertime already? He stretched. What he wouldn't give for a gaming chair and wall-mounted TV.

The excited sounds of voices came from next door and he heard them go out into the hall. Would there be any dinner left for him? He rushed towards the dining room.

Entering, Garrison saw a buffet of food that all smelled divine. He filled his plate until it heaped. There was no way he could get this to his room without spilling, so he sat down on the empty side of the long table nearest the door. An old man sat next to him, as though he sat there every day. Garrison inched away on the bench. Should he move? Was this the man's spot? Mae sat down on Garrison's other side, boxing him in. Garrison felt suddenly claustrophobic.

The old man called out to a woman about his same age. "Rebecca, my darling."

The woman, who just came into the dining room, blushed.

"Please, you two, not before I've eaten," said Tuck, sitting across the table from Garrison.

"One day, you'll understand," said Rebecca. She sat next to the old man and gave him a quick kiss.

"Doubtful," Tuck muttered.

Mae rolled her eyes. "Sam, were you able to fix that slow drain?"

The old man nodded. "Unfortunately, I fear it's a temporary fix. They are old cast-iron pipes, after all."

"Well, at least that's something."

Rebecca chimed in. "Whoever could have guessed that Sam would have a talent for plumbing."

It went on like that. Mae complained. Rebecca complimented. Sam gave updates and Tuck cracked jokes. It was like they were a family. Garrison felt part of it and separate from it, all at the same time. He pushed his food around his plate.

"Not hungry, dear?" asked Rebecca. She immediately reached across Sam to feel Garrison's forehead.

"I'm okay," he mumbled, pulling away. He shoved a forkful of potato into his mouth.

"Don't worry about him, Rebecca," Tuck said. "He's just worn out from playing God to small mindless creatures."

Rebecca looked horrified. "Tuck! What do you mean?"

Tuck shrugged.

Rebecca looked at Garrison. So did Mae and Sam. Garrison wished a hole would open up that he could disappear into. "Do you mean my video game?" he finally asked.

"Oh," said Rebecca, looking relieved. Which didn't make sense to Garrison, but he didn't know how to ask about it. The table was quiet after that. Garrison felt like it was somehow his fault.

When Tuck emptied his plate and excused himself, Garrison watched him go. It seemed fine until a few minutes later. Garrison turned towards the hall. Had he heard something? A whisper of...it wasn't a voice. He stood up.

"Is everything okay?" Rebecca asked.

Garrison looked at her. She and Sam were staring. Mae was looking at her plate, although her expression seemed to be amused for some reason. Garrison nodded and cleared his dishes. He wanted to get back to his room.

Garrison stood outside the door, looking at it. It appeared normal. No bucket balanced on top. Garrison just had a feeling though. Something about Tuck.

He swung the door open which creaked slightly. The stale air wafted out to him. Yet, everything appeared normal. Garrison stepped inside, roaming around the entire room and bathroom — no Tuck, no mysteriously moved items. Even the faucet in the bathroom ran crystal clear.

Garrison shook his head. He was being paranoid. He jumped onto his bed, grabbing his game on the way. The unit beeped. He looked closely at it and the battery icon was red. Then the unit turned off completely.

Garrison let out a swear word. He dug in his bag for the charger and plugged it into the wall.

He sat back on his bed again, staring out the window. It was just starting to get dark. He could barely see the trees at the edge of the farm, they were just shadows against the sky. It looked a lot like the newest level in his video game. He shivered. Then he told himself he was being stupid. He went to his bag and took out the book his mom made him pack. He fell asleep before reading all of the first page.

The next morning, Garrison crept into the kitchen early, hoping to snag some breakfast without having to go into the dining room.

Unfortunately, Mae was at the stove. "Omelet?" she asked, barely glancing at him.

He shrugged, trying to look innocent.

He watched her crack an egg into another pan — the largest brown egg he ever saw. There were more eggs on the counter, all of them tan with deep brown speckles. Each egg was also a slightly different size than the one next to it. Bizarre, Garrison thought.

"Those are fresh," Mae said, watching him. "I found where the hens were laying them."

Garrison nodded, not really caring.

"I know I probably shouldn't let them roam, but they like it," she said, expertly folding the egg pancake around a cheesy filling before sliding it onto a plate. "They lay more eggs," she added, as though Garrison was arguing the point. "And they keep the insect population down. I ensure all the eggs I serve are fresh, though." She handed him the plate and waited.

"Looks...fresh," he muttered.

Someone laughed from the doorway. It was Tuck.

"Here's one for you too," Mae said, holding out another plate.

Tuck took it, saying a quick, "Thanks. You're funny," he said to Garrison as they went into the dining room.

"Why?" Garrison asked as they sat. "I don't get it."

"Exactly!" Tuck forked eggs into his mouth.

Garrison ate a few bites himself. "Thought you were mad at me."

Tuck shrugged. "Today's a new day."

No one else sat by them, although a few people came close. They greeted Tuck, moving towards the table until they saw Garrison. Then they changed direction.

Garrison put his head down so he didn't have to watch. Once he was done, he ran back to his room. He picked up his portable game and powered it up.

Nothing.

He went over to the charger and plugged the game back in. No flash of the logo on screen. No small lightning bolt.

"Why does nothing work?" he asked the empty room.

He jiggled the cord, moved the charger to a different outlet and tried banging the entire unit against his palm, not that he really expected that to work. He looked at his cell phone charger, but it was the wrong type. He went to find Mae.

She wasn't in the dining room or the kitchen. He heard a loud noise outside and turned in time to see a giant riding lawn mower going by. He ran after it.

"Mae!" He ran in front of the mower.

She stopped the red metal beast. "What? What's wrong?"

"My game isn't charging."

Mae just stared at him.

Thinking she didn't understand, he continued. "I can't play my video game. It's dead and the charger doesn't work. I need a new one."

Mae shook her head. "Unbelievable," she muttered. She started the mower back up.

"But...can't you take me to a store or something?"

"No stores around here," she yelled over the engine.

"But...I know my mom went through a town on the drive."

"Can't." She shook her head. "I have to finish my chores. Find something else to do." She drove off, covering him with lawn dust.

Garrison stomped back into the house, letting the kitchen door bang closed behind him. In his room, he slammed the hallway door. Opened it, and slammed it once more. It just wasn't fair. He looked around the mauve lacy room. He wanted to tear every inch of flowered wallpaper down.

He went out into the hall. The house had a hush about it. Sometimes he heard a fan on as he passed a door. Sometimes there was quiet talking, but he couldn't make out any of the words.

Outside, there wasn't much to look at. He kicked a stone or two in the unpaved driveway. It scared a few of the chickens who ran behind the barn. He followed them, squinting in the bright sunlight, but they were quick, and he didn't intend to catch them. The barn interested him. It was large and red with a blue-gray roof. He ducked inside for a look.

The barn's only light came from the sun filtering through gaps in the wood, and a few strategic windows. There were wooden stalls, but no animals. The smell of hay lingered, reminding Garrison of a pumpkin farm he visited once on a school trip.

He walked along. One of the larger stalls housed an old car, partially covered by a tarp. The parts Garrison could see were deep blue with shiny silver accents. Judging by the dust on the tarp, the car had been there a long time.

He kept going and something rubbed against his leg. Glancing down, he saw a white and black cat leaning against his shin. It rubbed its face against his leg again, its long whiskers tickling. Garrison reached down and rubbed its head. "Hey there, kitty."

It immediately began to purr. He stroked its back and behind its ears, avoiding the one missing a chunk. "What's the other guy look like? Huh? Tough kitty."

He straightened up and continued walking. The cat followed. At one point, it ran ahead and darted into a hole in the stall door. Garrison looked over the top. There were lots more cats. Most were lounging on blocks of hay, but a few were rolling around, grabbing at each other. There were even three little kittens, two white and one gray. The two white ones were crouched down low, staring at a small insect. Garrison smiled.

He looked around for the latch to open the stall door. Unfortunately, the moment he opened it, the door made a loud creaking sound. Cats jumped everywhere. They shot past his bare legs, setting his skin tingling. He swayed a bit, dizzy at how they squeezed through tiny holes and leapt high, balancing on inch-wide boards until they ran out of sight. Even the kittens buried themself in the hay. Garrison shook his head, disappointed, and shut the stall door.

Further down, there was another interesting stall. It was full of stuff. Garrison shifted some of the things, and there, behind a rusty wheelbarrow, was a bike. It wasn't exactly Garrison's style. It was purple, with a long white seat covered in blue stars. On the front hung a plastic basket decorated with flowers. But, a bike meant freedom. He might even be able to make it to town. He could buy a new power cord. Or at least see if there was internet.

He examined the bike again. Like his bedroom, it was so overly feminine, it almost hurt to look at it. Plus the tires were flat.

"What are you doing?"

Garrison jumped. "Nothing," he said automatically. He turned to see Tuck coming closer, inspecting the bike.

"Want to help me burn the trash?"

"You burn the trash?"

Tuck nodded. "Mae lets me do it. I like fires."

Garrison looked away, trying to avoid eye contact.

"Not in a crazy way," said Tuck, seeming to read his thoughts. "I'm not going to set the house on fire or anything. But out here, we don't have regular trash pick up, so we burn the paper goods and stuff. I like bonfires, so Mae lets me do it."

Garrison still didn't meet his eyes. "I think I'll just go for a bike ride."

"On a girl's bike?" Tuck asked. "But the tires are flat."

Garrison looked at the bike again. It was definitely a girl's bike. An *old* girl's bike. He wondered if it was his mom's. Stuck away in the barn when she was too old for it. And was his video game worth the embarrassment of being seen on it. "I need to find a pump," he said to Tuck.

"But why bother? There's nothing to see for miles but fields."

Garrison flipped the bike over onto the seat and spun the wheel. It was surprisingly smooth. He rummaged around the stall, looking for a foot pump, but didn't see one. He decided to go back to the stall with the car and try there.

When he lifted the edge of the tarp on the car, he sneezed. It was even dustier than he expected.

"No pump. Oh well," Tuck said.

Garrison ignored him. There was a doorway in the back wall of the stall, behind the car's right bumper. He headed towards it. As he stepped through, his mouth fell open.

It was a shop. There were long wooden benches with adjustable clamps, massive saws and bright red tool boxes. The walls were covered in brown pegboards, filled with a jigsaw puzzle of metal levels, T squares, hand saws, wrenches and hammers. Glass jars were arranged neatly on a shelf that ran the length of each bench. They glittered with various screws, nails, bolts and washers. "Wow," Garrison breathed.

"Lawrence was quite the handyman," Tuck said, obviously following him.

"Who was Lawrence?" Garrison asked, picking up a round blade with wicked looking teeth. It must be a spare for one of the saws. He suddenly registered the unnatural silence behind him and looked up.

Tuck had a strange expression on his face. "You don't know...your own grandfather?" He stumbled over the words.

"Oh." Garrison returned to the blade. "That Lawrence. Yeah. I guess I forgot. He died a long time ago. Before I was born." He tried to keep his voice casual, but the moths fluttered. Should he have remembered his grandfather's name? Was this another thing that made him weird? He glanced at Tuck to see if he was judging him.

Tuck made a non-committal noise and flipped through some spare light switches on a bench.

Garrison wondered how Tuck knew his grandfather. But then realized Mae must have told Tuck about him. That made sense. Looking at Tuck, he seemed barely a year or two older than Garrison. He couldn't have met...it took a moment for Garrison to think of the name again...Lawrence.

Eventually, Garrison found an old foot pump in a wooden crate. It was a little rusty, but worked. He took it over to the bike, and a few sweaty minutes later, the tires were firm and rideable. He went inside the house to grab the cash his mom gave him for emergencies and his cell phone. Perhaps closer to town, he would get a signal.

He was just pushing off down the driveway when Tuck shouted to him. "Wait, where are you going?"

Garrison slowed, but didn't stop. "To find the town we passed on the way here."

Tuck reached out and took hold of the bike. His grip was tight and stopped the bike short. Garrison slammed into the handlebars. "Dude! What the heck?"

Tuck was shaking his head. "You can't go."

Garrison pushed at Tuck's hands. "Why?"

"Because...you just can't. The town is...dangerous."

"The woods are dangerous, the town is dangerous. What isn't dangerous around here?"

"The house."

Garrison shook his head. "Relax. I grew up in the city. I'll be fine."

"No."

Garrison gave Tuck a look. "Are you going to tattle on me to Mae?"

Tuck's jaw clenched.

"Then just leave me alone."

CHAPTER 4

Garrison stopped at the crest of yet another hill. He was breathing heavily and sweat rolled down his spine. He was beginning to think this wasn't a good idea.

All around were fields of fledgling corn plants and the sun was a heat lamp. He rubbed his face with his hand.

Suddenly, out of nowhere, came a loud HONK! Garrison's heart stuttered. Tires skidded on gravel right behind him. He turned to see a pickup truck swerve in his direction and then quickly around. There were several more honks, the men inside the cab laughing and pointing.

Garrison leaned on the handlebars, hoping he wouldn't pass out from the heat or the local crazies. He debated going back. The house might be weird, but at least no one was trying to scare him to death. Ultimately, it came down to the fact that there was nothing to do without his video game. He couldn't face an entire summer of being bored. He got back on the bike.

It was another 20 minutes before his destination was in sight. He pedaled on, passing houses and empty playsets. No one was outside, anywhere. The street ended with an intersection and Garrison saw a convenience store opposite. "Finally!" he yelled to no one. He raced across the street and parked the bike just outside the front windows. His was the only bike, but there were a few cars in the parking lot. He pushed through the glass door.

Inside, the store looked like any other — racks of chips, coolers full of drinks, brightly colored slushie machines, bags of candy. He felt at home and started wandering up and down the aisles. The air conditioning felt amazing too. He wasn't the only one who thought so. There were quite a few people spread throughout the store, talking and browsing leisurely. He pulled out his cell phone. One bar never looked so good, but who should he call? There were only two names in his contacts. And he knew his father wouldn't answer. He tapped Mom. He smiled when it began to ring. Maybe she would change her mind about coming to get him. Maybe she could FedEx him a charging cable. By the third ring, he knew she wasn't going to answer. She never took this long. Then her voicemail greeting started.

> *You've reached Rachel Redapple. By the time you hear this, I'll be in Bolívar, Venezuela. I know, isn't it exciting! Unfortunately, I'm not getting coverage there, so please email me. Adios!*

Venezuela, Garrison thought. He didn't know how far away that was, but it felt far. He hung up and opened the email app on his phone. It was web-based and sluggish, but he finally got a new message to open.

Hi Mom.
At the store now. My video game charger broke.
Rode an old purple bike here. Was it yours?
Mae was too busy.
I don't get internet at the house. It's so boring.
And weird.
Better go.
Luv you.
Garrison

He hit send and immediately regretted it. He probably sounded dumb. He didn't email much. Mostly texted.

"Can I help you?" The words came from behind him and felt more like an accusation than a question. Garrison turned around.

Standing there was a tall, thin woman with white curly hair and thick brown glasses. Her arms were crossed over her chest, but Garrison could still see her employee badge — BONNIE. "If you aren't buying anything, then you need to leave," she said.

Garrison swallowed his comment about all the other people who seemed to be just hanging out. Instead, he said, "I...I'm looking for a charging cable."

"This way," said Bonnie. She led him up to the checkout where a cashier, another old woman, was helping a customer. Bonnie turned back to him. "All the cables we have are right here." She pointed to a small plastic display of mini USB cables and cigarette lighter adapters. The one slot for USB C was empty.

"Do you have any more of those?" He pointed to the tag.

Bonnie crossed her arms again. "What you see is what we have." She considered him. "Who are you here with?"

Garrison hesitated, but decided it couldn't hurt to answer. "No one."

"All minors need to be with an adult." She pointed to a sign on the glass window Garrison didn't notice when he came in. It was plain white paper and the words written in marker read:

NO LONE MINORS. NO HORSEPLAY.
NO BACKPACKS.

Before Garrison could say anything, his attention was caught by the cashier. "$15!" She shouted it so loudly, Garrison winced. The very thin man wearing paint-splattered jeans and sweatshirt didn't though. Instead, he pulled out a brown leather wallet stuffed with cash. He thumbed through it, handing her a few bills.

"You're not from here," said Bonnie, "so who are you staying with?"

The paint-splattered man took two packs of cigarettes off the counter. Without a single word, or even a nod, he headed for the door. Garrison watched him while he answered. "My grandmother. Mae Redapple."

It was as though everyone sucked in their breath at the same moment. Goosebumps sprang along Garrison's neck. Had the air conditioning kicked into high gear? He looked around. Dozens of eyes were staring. Not just staring, but glaring at him.

"You need to move along," said Bonnie. "We obviously don't have what you want."

"I don't...wait, what?" was all Garrison could manage.

"She said, GET OUT," yelled the cashier. "Mae ain't welcome here, either are you." She narrowed her eyes and Garrison could feel the air drop a few more degrees. The staring crowd was muttering to each other. Garrison thought he heard the word crazy. He backed towards the door, wondering what was wrong with these people. Clearly, Mae did something to annoy them. He wondered if she tried to give them interior design advice. That might do it.

He walked out to the bike and threw his leg over. He looked towards the store, but immediately regretted it. The people inside were still giving him hostile stares. A man extended a knobby old finger and thrust it away several times, a clear gesture for him to go. What could Mae have done to so many people? Garrison got on the bike and rode away.

He chose a street at random. There hadn't been one friendly face there. Not one person defending Mae. And the word crazy. Was it crazy that her grandson would come to the store alone? Or did they think Mae was crazy? She certainly wasn't a warm and fuzzy grandmother, but crazy? There was no evidence of that.

He noticed a playground to his right. The yellow, blue and red structure was kidless, but offered a lot of shady areas where he could think. Wiping sweat from the bridge of his nose, he steered towards it, cutting through the parking lot of a large building.

"Nice bike." The voice came out of nowhere, startling Garrison. He jerked the handlebars and the bike's front wheel slid on some loose gravel. The bike went down sideways, taking him with it. His elbow and bare right leg took the brunt of the asphalt. Pain shot through them, igniting his anger. He looked up, an insult ready on his lips. It died instantly.

Staring at him was a group of teenage boys, only a few feet away, in the shade of the building. They were perched on an old living room couch that looked ridiculously out of place in a parking lot. Around the couch were dozens of skateboards. Garrison groaned. The boy in the center of the couch smiled, drawing Garrison's attention. He spoke and Garrison realized it was the same voice as before. "The glitter really brings out your eyes."

All the boys laughed.

"Yeah," agreed Garrison, forcing himself to smile. He pushed the bike off of him and stood. He tried not to rub at his elbow too much. Instead, chest expanded as far as it would go, he said, "It was an emergency." Garrison forced a chuckle. "A video game emergency."

"Video game, huh?" The middle boy stood and came towards Garrison. "Fancy Switch, I bet. Or maybe a VR? Never seen one of those around here."

Garrison's heart began to race, but he stood his ground. When the rest of the boys stood too, Garrison's treacherous stomach nearly hit reset on breakfast.

The middle boy stopped a bit more than an arm's length from Garrison. "Where you from?" he asked. His eyes were dark, unfriendly.

"Uh, Chicago," Garrison said, hoping he would be impressed. "I'm visiting my grandmother." That was good, Garrison thought. Make sure they know someone was waiting for him. "But my game died. The only way to get to the store was this stupid little girl's bike." He forced another laugh.

"GrandMOTHER?.. How proper." The middle boy sneered and the others guffawed. "So this *grandmother* of yours. She the one in the green house? What's her name—" He snapped his fingers.

"Barb North," said one of the other boys.

"Yeah, old lady North. You her grandson?"

Garrison shook his head. He wondered for a moment if these boys would have the same reaction to Mae's name as the adults. Maybe it would buy him some respect if he told the truth. He decided to go for it. "Mae Redapple."

There was a collective gasp.

"Murderous Mae?" asked one of the boys.

Garrison could feel his eyebrows shoot up at that.

"Dirk, shut it," said the middle boy. He dropped the sneer and considered Garrison. "So. What's it like?"

Garrison eyed them. "What is what like?"

The boy rolled his eyes. "The Wagon Wheel farm. Is Redapple as crazy as people say?"

Garrison tried for a sarcastic smile, like he was in on the joke. "Crazy. Right."

Another boy spoke. "Does that mean it's true? She hears voices?"

Dirk talked over him. "They say she killed her husband, but no one could prove it. Not without a body." The middle boy nodded, crossing his arms.

Garrison realized he was in over his head. He glanced around. The parking lot led to a street at the other end. Maybe he could make a run for it. The boys had skateboards, but he had a bike. That would be faster, right?

"You aren't planning to leave, are you? We were just getting to know each other." The middle boy put his chin down and winked at Garrison. It must have been a signal, because the rest of the boys all smiled at once. It wasn't a nice sight.

Garrison gripped the handlebars. He was about to push down on the pedals when they surged forward. Garrison closed his eyes, knowing it was too late. They were too close. He expected a blow to the stomach, someone to grab his arm. Instead, he heard yelling. He opened his eyes. All the boys were on the ground! "F-ing loose stones," the middle boy shouted. "Dirk. Get off me."

Garrison didn't hesitate any longer. He took off. Pushing down hard on the pedals, he tried to put as much distance as possible between himself and the boys. He heard skateboard wheels on the pavement and stood up to pedal even faster.

Movement caught Garrison's eye between two buildings. It was Tuck — waving at him. Garrison veered in that direction.

As he got close, Tuck backed up into the alley behind him, and Garrison followed. It opened on the other side to Main Street. They crossed it, turned right and stopped in another alley. Garrison leaned over the handlebars. He could barely breathe.

"Those. Boys," Garrison panted. "Who..."

"No idea," Tuck said, peering around the corner to the street. "Coast is clear. Come on."

Garrison didn't know what to say. Those were just some boys, not like a notorious street gang. Of course, what would a street gang be doing in the middle of nowhere? They were so quick to jump him. It made him wonder if the video game talk wasn't a good idea. If not for the loose stones — well, he knew he was *super* lucky.

They left the alley, Garrison walking the bike. Should he thank Tuck for following him? He glanced over. Tuck wasn't even looking at him. He was doing something strange, however. Every block or so, he waved his hand like he was swatting a fly. But there were no flies. Not here, on the road, in this heat. Garrison's head buzzed.

Movement caught Garrison's eye. His heart skittered. He expected to see the boys or another hostile grownup. It was just an empty plastic bag. The thing was caught on a fence and struggling in the slight breeze. Garrison didn't relax. He scanned the street. Curtains may have twitched in a few houses, but it could also have been his imagination.

They continued to walk. The houses grew few and far between, until finally, they left the last one behind and were surrounded only by cornfields.

Tuck finally spoke. "Let's take the shortcut."

Garrison looked around. "Where?"

"Through the fields."

"Are they Mae's?"

"No."

Garrison thought about the store, about the skateboard gang. "What if we get caught trespassing?"

"Then you better run." Tuck walked into the row between knee-high cornstalks. Garrison stood on the road for a moment. It must be a good shortcut because Tuck made it to town, walking, only 15 or so minutes after Garrison got there biking. There were no people in sight on the road or the field and the only house was a couple miles further up. It didn't show signs of being occupied either. He made his decision and followed Tuck into the fields.

CHAPTER 5

When Mae's house came into sight 20 minutes later, Garrison breathed easier. He put the bike back in the barn and hid it behind an old mattress. He wouldn't be using it again. Stepping outside, he looked around the farm. It felt different somehow. More welcoming. Except for a crowd of people in the grass near the trees. Usually, they congregated on the porch, not the grass. Plus, there was a hum in the crowd — excited, but tinged with high-pitched panic.

Tuck walked towards the group, and Garrison followed. Just at the outer edge, Garrison stopped. The tension was so thick; it felt like a wall.

Tuck continued forward and onlookers stepped aside for him, which Garrison felt was strange. Tuck was a teenage boy, and they were adults. As Tuck got to whatever was at the center, he knelt on the ground. Was that an arm sticking out from under a cloth? Garrison took an involuntary step forward for a better look. He saw someone on the grass, their face turned away. Long reddish-brown hair spilled across the ground. A tan coat was draped over the body like a blanket, but it didn't cover the arms or legs. All bare and covered in bruises.

"We need to get her inside." Garrison recognized Rebecca's voice, despite there being a tremble to her words.

"Wait!" someone shouted. "We know nothing about her. She could be an enemy."

"A child, Paul?" challenged Sam. He sounded furious. "Besides, she's been beaten."

He said no more.

Someone else asked the question Garrison was wondering. "She is still alive, then?" There was a pause, but then Rebecca's words came louder than ever. "Her pulse is strong."

"Mae," Sam said loudly. "You are the keeper. It is your decision."

Garrison looked around for Mae. He hadn't seen her in the crowd. He still didn't, but he heard her voice, firm and certain. "She is hurt and needs our help." Protests began at once, but Mae raised her voice to drown them out. "She is innocent until proven guilty." The protests dropped to stubborn whispers.

With some prompting from Rebecca, a large man picked up the body. Rebecca kept the edges of the coat tight and Garrison wondered if the girl was naked beneath. That made him gulp.

The crowd parted wider. Garrison ran to the side as Mae came into view, marching towards the porch in her black boots. The large man followed her with his strange bundle. He stepped in an indentation, causing him to jerk. The girl's head turned and Garrison sucked in a breath. It was indeed a girl, one that couldn't be much older than himself. Her face was pale, but there was purple around her eyes and her lip was bleeding.

"Damn fools," someone muttered.

Garrison glanced back. Most of the crowd was dispersed, or talking. Only one person was staring after the girl — the stocky blonde man who complimented Tuck's shocking wallet.

"Paul!" someone yelled. The blonde man turned. He nodded and joined a small group.

Rebecca, Sam, and Tuck were following the large man carrying the girl. Garrison didn't hesitate. He rushed after them.

It would have been too difficult for the large man to carry the girl up the cramped kitchen stairs, so they took the main staircase, Mae still leading the way. Garrison hesitated for a moment. Going upstairs was against Mae's rules. Of course, she took most of them back. Maybe she just forgot to mention going upstairs. He decided to follow and held his breath as he reached the top. But the upstairs hallway looked very much like the one below, creamy white, with doors all along the walls. Why didn't Mae want him up here? He caught up to the small group, stopping near Tuck.

Mae opened a door along the hall and stepped back. She motioned for the man holding the girl to go in. Rebecca followed. Sam stopped beside Mae and they both looked into the room.

"How do you think she got through?" Sam asked Mae quietly.

Mae shook her head. "Perhaps the boundary is failing."

"Impossible."

"Can you think of another explanation?"

Sam was quiet for a moment. "Not likely ones. Still, I think we should test the boundary, you and I."

Mae nodded.

"We might also want to set a watch tonight."

Mae sighed. "This isn't an army barracks."

"Be that as it may. Things are not right. The more advance warning we get of...well, anything, the better."

Mae scrubbed her face with her hand. "How long?"

"I should think a few days will tell us what we need to know."

Mae nodded. Then she locked eyes with Garrison. Her mouth thinned.

"Uh oh," Tuck muttered. Garrison could feel Tuck take a step away from him. A large step.

Mae came forward. "I told you not to come up here," she yelled.

"But I thought...you said I could explore—"

"You're grounded. No video games. No freedom. In fact, I'm locking you in." She practically pushed Garrison down the stairs to his room. He went without a word, not liking that look in her eye.

Mae was true to her word. Garrison barely made it inside his bedroom when she slammed the door. Garrison heard a small click. He reached out and tried the knob. It turned, but didn't open. He pounded his fist against the door. This was completely unfair. He should tell his mom. He pulled his phone out of his pocket, but the one bar he had in town was gone. Nothing would go through. He threw the phone onto the bed. He could feel tears coming. How could his mom just leave him like this? With Mae. She was crazy.

As crazy as people say? The words echoed in his mind. *Murderous Mae.* He pushed them away, swiping at his eyes, and walked to the window.

The sill was low to the ground, with no screen. He could probably escape through it. But where would he go? Town was not an option. Even if he lied now and told them he was Barb North's grandson, a bunch of people knew the truth. And what was Sam talking about — advanced warning? Mae being a keeper? This was just a farm, a hobby farm at that, not a commercial farm. Nothing made any sense.

Garrison looked out across the grass to where a slightly taller and wilder area began. That led into dense woods, full of dark shade. It was obvious that this was the boundary. Yet there was no fence. The girl could have just walked in. Or been dumped. Garrison gulped. That was a horrible thought. The image of her laying there, her body naked and bruised, formed in his mind. Something in his chest tightened and broke. Warm ooze seemed to spill out. It was a strange sensation, full of anger, but also caring. And maybe something else. He wondered if her hair would feel silky, if her skin would make his fingers tingle as he touched it? He shook himself. What was happening to him?

CHAPTER 6

She felt them lay her down. Felt the soft hands tuck a blanket around her, but she hadn't wanted to open her eyes. She just wanted to go back to where there was no pain, no thought, no betrayal. So she had. But this time, her eyelids didn't feel so heavy. Her mind was working better too, wondering what time it was and where she was. She decided it was time to wake up.

She found herself in a small room. The walls were robin egg blue, with ornate trim painted slightly darker. She could hear muffled voices as though there were people around, but not close by. The air smelled like cooking and her stomach growled.

She tried to sit up, but winced instead. Pulling the blanket back, she saw all the bruises — chest, abdomen, arms. Tears sprung to her eyes and she let them fall. She was in pain, all because of — her mind put up a wall and she could not remember who. She pushed at the obstacle, ramming her fists against it. Anger made her will strong, and the wall gave way, but there was nothing behind it. Her mind was suddenly empty.

She forced herself to sit up then, gritting her teeth at the pain. The room was small with basic furniture. A wooden dresser was on the wall to her right, topped with a large mirror. Ornate wooden embellishments adorned each of the three large drawers. Beside her single bed was a window with lace curtains and she could see a bit of grass beyond. It looked like she was on the second story.

To her left, along the wall, stood a small desk wedged in the space between the bed and the far wall. It was on long spindly legs, and above the surface rose two shelves of tattered, hardcover books. Also in that direction was another door. It stood slightly ajar, showing a small washroom with a toilet.

There was a knock on the bedroom door, directly opposite her and the bed. She could barely pull the blanket up over her naked body when it began to open. An older woman came in. She was wearing a long skirt, loose shirt and vest. The collection of beaded and leather bracelets along her wrists jangled pleasantly as she moved.

"Oh, hello, dear," she said, squatting down to look the girl in the eyes. "I'm so glad you're awake. I feared a concussion." The wrinkles around her brown eyes were deep, but in a kind way, and her white hair curled into loose waves. It was cut in a bob style that suited the woman, making her both beautiful and motherly at the same time. "How do you feel?" she asked.

"Hurt." The girl startled at her own voice. It was low and hoarse, not at all the voice she thought would come from her mouth. It made her frown.

"Understandable. I don't suppose you remember who did this to you?"

The girl thought about it, but the space in her mind remained stubbornly unresponsive.

"That's very common," the woman soothed. "The events leading to trauma are often forgotten, at least for a time." She patted the girl's hand. "The mind protecting itself. It's alright. What is your name?"

"It's…" Panic flooded the girl's system, splashing cold onto her skin and into her stomach. She pulled her knees up to the chest. "Oh, god. I can't remember."

The woman's eyes went sad, but she smiled. "Don't fret, love. It will return. Here." From a hidden pocket in her skirt, she produced a small, bound book in teal leather and a mother-of-pearl pen. "I brought you a journal to write in. Just jot down everything you remember. It will all come back. I promise."

The girl swallowed, anxiety a tasteless lump in her throat. Her stomach gurgled. In the empty space of her mind came the image of her favorite treat — an oval of fried dough covered in cinnamon and sugar. Her mouth watered, and she swore she could smell it.

"I bet you're hungry," the woman said with a sympathetic frown. "I'll go ask for a tray of food to be sent up. And I'll bring you back a nice dress too, something loose you can slip on."

Suddenly remembering her nakedness, the girl clutched the blanket tighter to her. How utterly embarrassing, she thought, to be found this way. Had something even darker happened to her? She glanced down between her legs.

"I don't think anything like that happened," said the woman. "No external evidence, anyway. I'm sorry, but I felt compelled to check. It's the healer in me. But how does it feel to you?"

The girl relaxed slightly. "Um, normal, I guess." It was a bit more her voice now, but still too low.

The woman nodded. She reached out and pushed some hair behind the girl's ear. "I'm Rebecca. And I'll do everything I can to help. Okay?"

The girl believed her.

"I'll be right back."

The girl watched her straighten up and leave, giving one last reassuring smile as she closed the door behind her. Ignoring the pain, the girl stood and crossed to the dresser. She looked at her naked body. There were plenty of bruises, like she was hit several times, but nothing else. Except, there, on the back of her shoulder. She turned, brushing her hair out of the way. There was a tattoo in bright red ink. Seven swords, like arrows, woven to shoot in all directions, rose from a ship at sea. It stood out like fresh blood on her light skin. Something about it made her catch her breath. It represented something, but what? She could remember the emotions associated with it, betrayal, but it once meant pride, too. She was so confused. There was one certain thing, however. She did not want anyone to see it. She let her hair drop back, blocking it.

When Rebecca returned, the girl was sitting on the bed again, wrapped in the blanket.

"Here, let's hope this fits," Rebecca said, holding up a simple rust-colored dress. "I brought you some underthings as well. I'll let you get dressed in private." Rebecca piled everything on the dresser.

The girl mumbled a thank you.

Rebecca looked towards the window and rubbed her hands together. She wondered what the woman was waiting for. Had she seen the mark on her shoulder when she examined her? Was she going to ask about it?

Rebecca took a deep breath and looked back with a tight smile. "The woman whose house this is would like to speak with you. Just be as honest as you can, alright, my dear? It will be fine. And try to get some rest in the meantime."

The girl watched her go, nerves making her skin tingle. She supposed it was normal for the owner of the house to want to talk to her. Or was it something more? Would she expect her to remember by then? It was all too much, too hard. The girl lay down and let the tears come, although whether they were for her present situation or her past, she didn't know.

Time went by and she found herself in that quiet, untethered state, on the verge of sleep. Her mind was wandering, showing her images of a perfect climbing tree, a vast bedroom filled with green velvet. It matches your eyes, someone said. Then there was a man. He was tall, even sitting down at the long polished table she saw next. The light was so dim; it was hard to see him, which was the way he liked it. Someone told her once that he only wore black suits, so he could better fade into the shadows. He liked to watch you.

The man turned his head, and she glimpsed of his crown of antlers. He still had the face of a stag, much to his irritation. Something changed, and suddenly, he was up close to her, the light nearly blinding. "There's only one way." The voice was deep and clear, but odd, coming from the deer head. He was so close, she could see the small brown hairs sprouting from his skin, smell the hide. She focused on his eyes — solid black and large enough for her to see her reflection. Was she wearing a tiara? The deer suddenly growled, "Your blood."

She opened her eyes on a gasp and sat up. What was that? Had she fallen asleep after all? She shivered. *Her blood.* The words rang in her head, in her heart. She got up and walked over to the dresser. She pushed the back of the dress down to see the tattoo. It was still there, still blood red. *Blood.* She didn't want to think about it, to know any of it.

She glared at the room, seeing now the smallness of the space. She felt enclosed. Focusing on the rumpled bed cover, she noticed intricate patterns sewn along the top and thick, handmade lace trim. She crossed back to the bed and fingered the lace. A memory of someone making it came to her, not this lace exactly, but one similar. She recalled smooth pale fingers holding white thread and a metal, leaf-shaped shuttle. Then the shuttle flashed quickly, above and below, above and below, over and over. It was a mesmerizing sight, the tatting. She looked up from the hands and the woman's face was intent. Counting.

"Mum." The girl said the word aloud, in the memory, and to the empty blue room. A strange mix of love and hurt rose with it — they were feelings she couldn't put reasons to, just felt. The emotions tossed her heart around in a hurricane. She slammed her fist on the bed. Tears bit at her eyes again, and she threw herself down. A mistake. Pain reminded her why she was here. Why she couldn't remember.

She looked over at the desk. The journal was lying open, blank. Perhaps she should do as the healer asked. Perhaps it would be good to write about what she saw, what she felt. She moved to the old wooden chair and sat, fingering the niches and scratches on the worn desktop. Who else sat here over the years, she wondered, writing, worrying. She picked up the pen. It seemed to have fragments of rainbows imprisoned in the lines of pearl. Around the pen's barrel was a ring of gold etching that looked like branches. Or antlers. With a sigh, she put the pen tip to paper and began to write.

She was still there, at the desk, when the knock came. Two brief solid taps. She stood up and faced the door. It did not open. "Enter," she said. The word came out firm and commanding, despite her raspy voice. She wondered why she said it that way. Why that word and not who is it or come in?

The person on the other side of the door opened it slowly. Another older woman, but not Rebecca. This one had a face like she lived on lemons. Her hair was pulled back tight and her eyes narrowed. She entered and tugged the door closed behind her. "Good evening," she said, her free hand returning to the tray of food she held. It smelled amazing. The girl's stomach did backflips.

The woman didn't smile, but continued in a matter-of-fact tone. "My name is Mae Redapple, and this is my home. Obviously, you're in a bit of a bad way, so you're welcome to stay for a while. You're safe here. It's one of the," she paused, "protected places."

The girl could see Mae watching for a reaction to those words, but she wasn't sure how to respond. The phrase *protected places* did have a resonance to it, as though she heard it before, but where?

Mae pushed her lips together. "Have you remembered your name?"

The girl gritted her teeth. Her name. She desperately wanted it. She looked at the mirror; large green eyes peered back. She stared harder, willing the image to say it, to tell her. "Carly," she said, and was pretty sure it was true. She looked back at Mae. "My name is Carly."

Mae nodded. "It's nice to meet you, Carly. Do you have a last name, sorry, surname?"

That made Carly feel uneasy. Something she couldn't quite remember stuck in her throat, making it difficult to swallow. It got worse when she noticed how Mae's eyes were gray, like silver discs. Carly couldn't think why it mattered. She knotted her hands into fists, frustrated.

"No rush," Mae said. She came forward and Carly stepped aside. Mae continued to the desk, pausing for a moment. Was she staring at the journal? Carly held her breath.

Mae pushed the journal aside to make room for the tray of food. When she straightened up, she opened her mouth as though to say something, but must have changed her mind. She crossed to the door instead. "I'm going to keep your door locked for now. We don't know who...what happened to you. And with the circumstances of the war, it's just safer. For everyone."

Carly didn't reply. Mae's words were reverberating in her brain. *War.* She barely noticed as Mae left, locking her in.

CHAPTER 7

Several hours had passed since Mae imprisoned him, and Garrison was hungry. His unfortunate trip to town and the subsequent appearance of the girl meant he missed lunch. He heard a noise at the door and stood, ready to tell Mae this was cruel and unusual punishment. There was a click and the knob turned. However, when the door opened, it wasn't Mae. It was Tuck.

He squeezed through and shut it again quickly. "Hello," Tuck said.

Garrison sat back down on his bed. "Hey."

"Mind if I come in?"

Garrison shrugged. "You're kind of already in."

"You know what I mean."

Garrison nodded to the empty bed on the other side of the room. Tuck went to it and sat down. "What's going on?" Garrison asked.

Tuck took out a deck of cards. "I was in town with you, remember? What makes you think I know?" He split the cards into two piles, angled them together and shuffled. The sight of cards flying together was mesmerizing.

Garrison pushed. "Who could have done that to a girl?"

"The question du jour."

"Yeah, but you must have a guess."

"Not a clue."

Garrison tried to read his expression. Tuck wasn't looking at him, but flipping a card over the backs of his fingers. It was impressive. "Where'd you learn to do that?"

Tuck put all the cards together and fanned them out in an arc. "My grandfather. Pick a card."

It was childish, but Garrison couldn't resist. He walked over and pulled a card from the middle. He held it up. "Two of diamonds."

"Great." Tuck put the cards back together and started cutting the deck, steadily adding more and more cards to his top hand, but still keeping them face down. "Okay, now I'm going to have you put it back. Say when."

Garrison waited until about half the deck was in Tuck's top hand. "When."

Tuck rolled his eyes and held out the pile. Garrison placed his card on top. He watched carefully as Tuck covered it with the rest of the deck. Garrison couldn't see any extra finger movements or markings.

Tuck snapped his fingers, then tapped the deck twice. He spread the cards out on the bed in a long line. "One of these cards will be different now." He pushed at them a bit.

Garrison saw immediately that one of the card backs was now red instead of blue. He smiled even before Tuck picked up the red card. "What was your card again?" Tuck asked.

"The two of diamonds."

Tuck did a cool flip twist to reveal the underside of the red card. Sure enough, it was the two of diamonds.

"That's pretty impressive," Garrison said.

"Watch. I'll do it again." Tuck put the red-backed two of diamonds on the bed, face down. Then he picked up the cards into one pile in his left hand and slowly drew them one at a time into his right. "Tell me when to stop."

"Stop."

Tuck picked up the last card on the top of the pile — the five of clubs. Then he put the deck back together and snapped, a sharp hard sound, followed by two taps. When he spread the cards out on the bed, there were only blue-backed cards.

Garrison glanced up at him. "Oops?"

Tuck held up a finger — *just one moment.* Without a word, but with a great flourish, he flipped over the red card set aside from earlier. It was now the five of clubs.

Garrison laughed. "How did you do that?"

Before Tuck could answer, the bedroom door swung open. This time, it was Mae. "Tuck," she said, glaring at him. It wasn't as cold as Garrison expected, and Tuck answered with an over-the-top smile that looked comical.

Then Mae turned to Garrison. "Listen, Garrison. I may have overreacted upstairs. I'm just trying to keep you out of it. Things around here...well, they aren't quite what you might expect. Safe even."

"Yeah. I can see that," he said. "Did you call the police? Do they know who did that to the girl?"

Mae looked to the side. "No. There are some..." she paused, considering, "extenuating circumstances."

Tuck snorted. "It's not like they'd come. They live in town."

That made Garrison pause. After his experience with the townspeople, he wasn't sure ANY of them would be friendly or helpful, even police officers.

"Anyway," Mae continued. "It's important you stay on the property, Garrison. You too, Tuck. Now, come on. It's dinnertime." She walked away.

Tuck rose from the bed, leaving the cards in a random pile. As he passed Garrison, he whispered, "Don't mention your trip to town."

"Why?"

Tuck didn't answer, but Garrison thought about it as he followed. Mae locked him in his room for simply going upstairs. What would she do if she found out he snuck off to town? Best not to find out.

There were people in the dining room when they arrived. Mae led them to where Sam and Rebecca were sitting, apparently waiting for them.

"Hello, dears," Rebecca said.

"Hi," replied Tuck. He winked at her.

She smiled.

Garrison wanted to ask her about the girl, about how she was doing. But how would Mae react to that? He glanced at her. She was using a knife to cut her salad into small bites. He felt someone's eyes on him and caught Tuck staring. They exchanged a look, and Tuck did a half-smile that made Garrison uncomfortable.

Tuck took a large bite and said, "So, Rebecca. How's your patient doing?"

The noise in the dining room stopped.

Garrison turned to the other tables. Everyone was staring at their plates. Did they all want to know about the girl?

Rebecca's smile lessened. "Oh, she's doing alright."

As though Tuck didn't notice the change in the room, he continued, "And who is she?"

"Unfortunately, remembering is a challenge at the moment."

"Amnesia?" Tuck commented. "Interesting."

Garrison thought he heard someone in the room murmur, "And convenient."

Rebecca sat up straighter. "It's completely normal. The mind wants to protect itself from trauma."

"Indeed," said Sam loudly. He put a hand lightly on Rebecca's back. Support.

Mae spoke up then. "Well, she has remembered her name, at least. Carly. Can't recall the rest yet, but we'll give it time." She paused. "Also, I have decided to keep her door locked."

Garrison stared at Mae. Was locking people in their rooms her solution to everything? He hoped not. Carly didn't even do anything wrong. Someone else beat her.

Then another thought occurred to him. A locked door kept people out as much as it kept people in. Interesting indeed.

Tuck gave Mae a mock salute. "Yes, Warden. Let this be a lesson to anyone who dare annoy you." Everyone in the dining room laughed.

Mae rolled her eyes at him. "Keep it up, Tuck, and you'll be clearing out the chicken coop."

Tuck put a hand on his chest like he was having a heart attack.

Garrison looked around. People were back to eating and talking. Whatever awkwardness the question about Carly brought up was over. He wondered if Tuck knew what he was doing or if it was an accident?

"Speaking of chickens," Tuck said, "do you remember when they got in the garden last year?"

Sam laughed. "It was a mess."

"A mess? They were artists. Garrison, I swear to you, one hen pecked a zucchini into the exact likeness of Mae."

Garrison laughed.

Mae waved a hand. "It looked nothing like me."

"It actually did," whispered Rebecca. She was laughing so hard that there were tears in her eyes.

After dinner, Garrison wandered out onto the back porch, Tuck beside him. The sky was bright pink and purple.

"So, what's your story?" Tuck asked.

"My story?" No one ever asked him that. He could tell Tuck the basics — his age, height, weight. But that wasn't really *his* story? He didn't quite know what to say. "I like video games," Garrison ventured. "Yeah. I'm really into open world games. My dad has this killer TV that makes you feel you're in them."

Tuck nodded, but didn't elaborate on the subject.

"Speaking of TVs, are there any here? I haven't heard a single one in any of the rooms."

Tuck shook his head. "There's no coverage."

"There's no cell coverage, no Wi-Fi, and now you're saying TVs don't work. What is this place, the Stone Age?"

"Close."

"Haha. But seriously."

Tuck shrugged.

"So what is there to do around here, then?"

"We find ways to amuse ourselves."

Garrison considered him. He remembered Tuck's shocking wallet when he first arrived and the red dye tablets. "Maybe you'll have to show me sometime."

Tuck grinned. "Maybe I will."

Garrison couldn't think of anything to say to that, so they fell into silence. He marveled at how it wasn't uncomfortable. He didn't feel as self-conscious as he did when he was at school and this happened. Did that mean he and Tuck were...friends? He could barely think the word.

The sun set so quickly, Garrison didn't know how it happened. One moment, it was light, and the next, the air seemed to darken. Sam came towards them from the yard. He was yawning. "You boys better turn in for the night."

"Mm-hmm," Garrison said.

Tuck nodded.

Neither moved, they just stared into the growing darkness.

"What do you see?" Tuck asked quietly.

Garrison glanced at him, forehead wrinkled. "Like out there?" He gestured to the backyard.

Tuck nodded.

Garrison looked. It was the same as it was before. "Grass. Bushes, trees, and stuff. Fireflies. What do you see?"

Tuck paused. His eyes moved along the property line. "Shadows. Lots of shadows."

It was an odd response. Garrison supposed there were shadows beneath the trees and bushes. Still, it was weird and Garrison didn't know what to say. The silence spread between them.

"Well, I guess I better find a place to sleep."

"You don't have one?"

Tuck shrugged. "I've been spare bed surfing."

"That's right. I'm staying in your room."

"Mm-hmm."

Garrison gulped. He could ask Tuck to use his spare bed, but what if it was weird? What if he said no? Garrison's stomach was ice, but each time he swallowed, drops of lava fell into it. He realized Tuck was staring at him. "Um. Well, there are two beds, if...I mean, I don't know."

"Thought you'd never ask. I'll grab my stuff and meet you there."

Garrison let out a big sigh as Tuck ran off. That was a relief.

He left the porch and headed to his room, now their room. Had he made a terrible mistake? What if Tuck was a horrible roommate? What if he was? Garrison rubbed his aching stomach.

It didn't take long for Tuck to arrive. He opened the door, holding a large suitcase, guitar, and wearing a leather messenger bag. His smile was huge and infectious. It was like this was a sleepover. Garrison supposed in some ways, it was. It would be his first. Garrison found himself smiling back.

CHAPTER 8

The next day, Garrison was waiting for Tuck outside on the side porch after breakfast. Tuck flew out the back door, handing him a popsicle. "Eat it quick. I swiped it when Mae wasn't looking."

Despite having just eaten, Garrison gulped down the cherry-flavored ice as they headed away from the house.

They headed towards the barn, hiding near the bushes to sneak the rest of their popsicles. "So, do you think Carly's remembered anything yet?" Garrison asked.

Tuck snorted. "Why do you care?"

Garrison shrugged. "No reason."

Tuck made a kissy noise.

"Shut up."

Tuck grinned. "You're obsessed."

"I am not." But Garrison was a little worried he was. He felt strange when he thought about the girl. Her image clung to his neurons.

"Mae asked me to take her lunch today."

"When?"

"At lunch."

"No, I mean, when did she ask you? I was with you all morning."

"Except when I snuck in for the popsicles."

"That's when she asked you?"

"Cornered me is more accurate."

Garrison considered. "Why did she ask you? Is there something I don't know?"

"Relax. She just thinks the girl will talk to me, since we're closer in age."

"But I'm close to her age, too."

"Sure you are."

"No, really, why did she ask you and not me?"

"In case you didn't notice, Mae's a bit protective of you."

Garrison gaped. Protective was not the word he would use.

"She's trying to keep you separate, away from what's going on. I think it's misguided. Which is why I am going to ask you to come with me."

Garrison knew his mouth was open again. No words came out, though. Was Tuck serious?

"Eat early and make sure Mae sees you leave. Go back to our room. Then sneak out and meet me outside Carly's door at 12:30."

Could he really get away with it? Garrison wondered. Because if Mae found out, she'd kill him. She would definitely lock him in his room again. But maybe he could help. Maybe Carly would tell him who hurt her and they could be brought to justice. "I'm in."

Tuck smiled, like he just announced checkmate.

Two hours later, Garrison was rushing up the main stairs. Tuck was already at the top, holding a tray with food. He let go with one hand to make an unnecessary hurry-up motion.

When Garrison got close, Tuck knocked on the door.

"Who is it?" asked Carly.

"Tuck and Garrison. We've brought you lunch."

"Oh."

There was a pause.

"May we come in?"

"Only if you have the key."

Tuck shrugged at Garrison as he pulled the key from his pocket. Garrison wondered why Mae trusted Tuck at all when he was so clearly...Tuck.

When Tuck unlocked the door, Garrison swung it open. The girl was sitting on her bed, cross-legged. Garrison's throat constricted. Her thick, coppery hair fell well past her shoulders. Her pale face was splattered with freckles, and her eyes were so green they looked almost unreal. Tuck walked past him and whispered in his ear, "Your drool is showing."

In the room, Tuck turned to Carly. "I'm Tuck. And that, well, he's Garrison. We're pleased to meet you."

Carly didn't look away from Garrison. In fact, her gaze was so intense, he felt himself blush.

"Um, hello?" Tuck asked. Garrison glanced at him. It was strange to hear Tuck at a loss for words. Tuck put the tray down on the dresser. He cleared his throat. "So, remember anything yet?"

Carly shook her head. "It's all disjointed images and feelings, really. But there is something...your eyes." She said this to Garrison. "They're just like the woman's. But now I remember." The girl's forehead wrinkled. "The sight. Silver orbs, no. But something with silver."

Tuck took an aggressive step forward. "We are not interested in any of that." His voice was hard, clipped. Garrison stared at him. So did Carly. It broke whatever spell she was under, and she focused completely on Tuck. "We want to know how you got here," he said.

"I told the healer; I don't know."

"Nonsense!"

Garrison couldn't take it anymore. He stepped in front of the girl, facing Tuck. "Dude. Back off."

Tuck turned to the door and his back moved like he was taking deep breaths.

Garrison pivoted in place and nearly melted into a puddle of goo when he saw Carly smile, just a little, at him. He coughed twice, but finally managed to say, "It's just that everyone is confused...and a little scared. Because this is—"

"One of the protected places," Carly finished. "Yes, I know."

It was Garrison's turn to be puzzled. That was not what he was about to say. "What does that mean?"

Carly looked at him. "It means the army can't get through."

Tuck butted in. "The army?"

Carly looked down. "Um...I think that's what it is. They attack smaller villages and farms. Take them over."

Tuck crossed his arms and gave her a disapproving look.

"Maybe that's not right. Oh, I don't know what's real anymore." The girl's voice cracked.

"It's okay," said Garrison. "Take your time. You were hurt. Do you know who did it?"

Carly shook her head again. "I keep seeing this nightmare figure of a deer, but that can't be right."

"A deer or a stag?" Tuck asked.

"Does it matter?" Garrison asked.

"Shhhh. Carly, a deer or a stag?" Tuck pushed.

"A stag, I think."

"And he beat you?"

"I'm not sure, but he was there. I think." She looked down at her bed. "I don't know for sure."

Garrison couldn't stand it anymore. "Tuck, I think that's enough. Let's just leave her to rest." He smiled at Carly.

Tuck nodded. "Feel better." Carly's gaze was stony when she nodded at him, a fact that made Garrison smile even more.

Garrison led the way out into the hall, Tuck following. Tuck pulled the door closed and locked it. Then together, they headed towards the main stairs.

"Tuck, what was that?" Garrison asked. He tried to keep his voice low. "Why were you being so mean to her?"

"I wasn't being mean. We were playing good cop, bad cop."

"What?"

Tuck stopped and turned to face him. "I was being the bad cop, so she would confide in you. And it worked." He started walking again.

Garrison ran after him. "What do you mean, it worked? She's obviously seeing things. I mean, a stag man? That's not logical. And an army taking over small villages and farms? Nothing like that is going on."

"Obviously," said Tuck, but he didn't turn around.

"Seriously, Tuck, were you just playing with her? Because that was cruel."

"We needed answers. I'll do anything for this place."

Garrison put his hand out to stop Tuck. "What does that mean?"

"It means this is my home. Mae, Sam, Rebecca — they'd all do the same for me."

Garrison felt the jealousy like a sword thrust. It pierced his stomach and drove itself upward into his heart, where it twisted. He wanted a group of people he would do anything for, who he knew would do anything for him. A family. For a moment, he hated Tuck for having it. But that was stupid. Tuck obviously didn't ruin it the way Garrison had. He deserved to be happy. "Got it."

"I need to go talk to Mae."

Garrison simply nodded.

Tuck's expression changed. He looked almost nervous. "Meet you back at our room?"

The *our* sent a guilty pang through Garrison's chest, a slightly happy one. He nodded. Tuck rushed off down the stairs, but Garrison waited there for a moment. The door behind him opened.

"Oh, excuse me," said Paul. "I'm just on my way out."

Garrison shook himself. "Yeah. Sorry about that." He left, returning to his room.

CHAPTER 9

Garrison filled his glass with water a second time. He didn't know how Tuck stood the heat. Garrison even offered to bring him out some water, but Tuck refused. So Garrison was inside alone. The early afternoon sun streamed in the kitchen window, making the off-white cabinets orange.

A phone rang. Garrison turned towards the sound. Two phones were attached to the kitchen wall. One was metal, a box with a round dial in the center, and one of those metal ear pieces you see in antique photos. He doubted it worked.

The ringing was coming from the other phone. White molded plastic with one of those curly cords running from the base to the handset. It made a tinny "brrring" sound.

Mae came rushing in and grabbed it. "Hello." In the pause at the other end, Mae turned to lock eyes with Garrison. "But how does anyone even know he's here?" Her eyes widened. "No. No, he hasn't been to town."

Garrison stared at his glass, avoiding Mae's eyes. Guilt sent a wave of acid crashing into his stomach.

"Here?" Mae asked. Garrison glanced up to see if she was angry. Mae's back was to him now, her hand curled into the cord. "Today?...I suppose. Yes. Fine. See you at three o'clock then." As she hung up, Mae put her forehead to the wall. Before she could turn and give him an angry look, he ran out the side door.

Garrison headed towards the barn. Tuck could usually be found there. As he walked, his mind was buzzing. Maybe he should have told Mae about taking the bike into town. But Tuck told him not to. Why was it even a big deal? So he got kicked out of the convenience store. So there was a gang of skateboard guys threatening him. Who even was that on the phone?

Tuck wasn't in the barn, but Garrison couldn't go back to the house. Not yet. He kept picturing the way the townspeople's eyes narrowed at the mention of Mae, how the boys called her murderous Mae, like it was a nickname. He sat on an old crate in the corner of a stall. Why did his mother abandon him here? Why did she have to go off to Timbuktu, or wherever she was? He wrapped his arms around his stomach and leaned forward. He wished his video game worked, or his cell phone. Anything! The guilt was etching his insides, and it burned. What was he going to do?

An hour or so passed, and he was still there, hunched on a crate. He had to do something. He wanted to find out who was coming to see Mae. That meant he had to go back to the house. He decided his best option was to sneak in the front door and hide in the study. That way, he could hear everything said in the front hall.

He left the barn and walked along the long gravel drive to the front of the house. There were a few people on the large front porch, fanning themselves. They ignored him. He didn't call out or wave, either. Inside the house, the big clock in the hall said 2:40. He sighed in relief and looked around. There were two wooden doors that could be closed to seal off the study from the house. Mae usually kept them open. Garrison pushed his way behind one of them, standing in the small triangle of space made behind it. He could see the front door and most of the foyer through the vertical gap beneath the door hinge. He waited there, listening. The clock counted down. Tick. Was he a minute closer to being sent away again? Tick. Where would he have to go this time? Tick. What was wrong with him that every place he went fell apart?

The doorbell rang at exactly three o'clock. Mae came down the hall and opened the front door.

A stocky woman in a black suit dress stood in the opening. "Ms. Redapple," she said. "I am Mrs. Ethelmeyer from the Department of Child Protective Services. We spoke on the phone. I appreciate your willingness to see me today." The words were nice, but the tone was clipped.

Mae stepped back, and Mrs. Ethelmeyer entered. Then she looked around. "As I said earlier, our role is to ensure children are safe and protected in the home. Our office received a call about your grandson, Garrison Johnson, apparently after a trip he took to town."

"Yes, you explained all that. Why couldn't we do this over the phone, though?"

"There were some disturbing accusations made. Therefore, I wanted to follow up in person."

Mae crossed her arms. "What kind of accusations?"

Mrs. Ethelmeyer stood straighter, but turned her gaze away from Mae. "I'm not comfortable saying."

"You mean saying that it's because of the allegations from 30 years ago? Because I was cleared. And it has nothing to do with my grandson."

"There is no need to be defensive, Ms. Redapple."

Garrison could see a muscle in Mae's jaw clench and unclench.

Mrs. Ethelmeyer cleared her throat and looked at Mae again. "I would simply like to speak with him, your grandson, that is. Just a brief chat."

Mae sighed. "Garrison," she called, turning to look at him through the gap in the door. "Come meet Mrs. Ethelmeyer."

Garrison swallowed the panic of getting caught, and stepped out from behind the study door. Mrs. Ethelmeyer made a startled noise and put her chubby hand to her chest, but she recovered quickly. She peered at him. "You are Garrison Johnson?"

Garrison nodded.

"Is there a place where we can talk privately?"

Garrison looked at Mae. She shrugged. "I'll go to the kitchen and make some coffee."

"Do you have tea?" Mrs. Ethelmeyer asked.

"Yes."

"Earl Grey?"

Mae nodded.

"I shall have that. No milk, of course."

Mae gestured to the study behind Garrison and turned away. He stared at her back for a moment, wishing she would stay, despite what Mrs. Ethelmeyer said. As though she could feel his stare, Mae turned her head. She gave him an encouraging, if weak, smile. Garrison felt just the tiniest bit better.

Mrs. Ethelmeyer walked towards him, drawing his attention. He stepped aside, thinking she may have pushed him out of the way. She glanced around at the bookshelves and photos. Then she took out a small black notebook and pen. She made a note. Then she sat on the sofa and indicated a chair opposite. "Sit, please."

Garrison sat.

"So, Garrison. You heard why I'm here then?"

"Yes. And I wasn't doing those things. Well, I was, but it's not how you said it."

"Then how would you describe it?"

"I was just in the store to get a charging cable for my video game. I wasn't loitering. And I wasn't running away. In fact, they kicked me out! When I told them I was Mae's grandson."

She gave him her full attention. "You call your grandmother by her first name?"

Garrison winced internally, but it was the truth. "Uh. Yeah." He couldn't think of anything else to say.

Mrs. Ethelmeyer just stared at him.

"Okay, fine," Garrison went on to fill the void. "I was riding the bike without a helmet, but my grandmother didn't know. I took it from the barn."

"She didn't notice you riding away on a bicycle in the middle of the day?"

"She was mowing the lawn. I made sure she didn't see me."

Mrs. Ethelmeyer wrote something down in the notebook. A few somethings judging by the scratching of her pen. Finally, she looked up. "And you're getting plenty to eat?"

Garrison relaxed a little. "Plenty. There's a ton of food around. Eggs, waffles, pancakes for breakfast, sandwiches and salads for lunch, and tons of options for dinner. Mae even makes pies and cakes for dessert."

She made another note. "And what do you do during the day?"

"Mostly, I hang out with Tuck. He's about my age and lives here."

"There's another boy here?" Mrs. Ethelmeyer's tone was light and non-threatening, setting Garrison immediately on edge.

Mae came in then with two mugs and a white teapot on a tray. "Earl Grey, no milk. I brought some lemon slices for you, though."

"Garrison says you have another boy staying with you. Who is he?"

"Ah." Mae quickly glanced at Garrison and back again. "There was a boy. The son of a friend of mine. They, the family that is, stayed with us for a bit. But they've gone."

"Tuck left?" Garrison shouted.

Mae turned and gave him a look, but he didn't understand what it meant. Through clenched teeth, she said, "He told me to tell you goodbye."

Garrison felt hollow.

"Excuse me, Ms. Redapple, but might I get some sugar?"

Mae gave Garrison another *look* and left. Mrs. Ethelmeyer scooted to the edge of her seat. "Now, Garrison. Tell me all about this young man. Tuck, I believe you called him."

Before Garrison could answer, the front door opened and closed. Tuck walked past the study.

"There," Garrison yelled, elated. "He's there. You can meet him yourself. Tuck!"

Tuck turned. He smiled at Garrison and then noticed Mrs. Ethelmeyer. "Fart nuggets!"

Before Garrison could respond to that, Tuck went on in a rush. "Don't tell her you can see me. Or anyone! Except Mae. Don't tell her anything about this place."

"But why?"

Tuck shook his head. "I knew Mae should have told you. I've been saying so for days. Listen, I can't explain everything right now with you gawking at me. But she can't SEE me. No! Don't repeat that. Just play this off as a joke."

Garrison felt like his brain was buffering.

Mrs. Ethelmeyer cleared her throat. "But why what?" She leaned this way and that, searching the hallway from her seat, as though Tuck wasn't standing right there. "Are you seeing him right now, dear?" she asked.

In Garrison's brain, an error message popped up. Failure to connect. "Ha," he said. "I gotcha. There's no one there." Garrison's voice wasn't natural, but he hoped she wouldn't notice.

"No one there?" Mrs. Ethelmeyer repeated.

Garrison swallowed. Was this the biggest mistake of his life? Should he just admit Tuck was standing there?

"You're staring at thin air. Pretended to see a boy who you claim was here for," she paused, her lips pulling into a tight, annoyed circle, "a joke?"

Mae came rushing back into the room. "Here's your sugar."

Mrs. Ethelmeyer eyed her. "Garrison was just telling me how Tuck is back."

Tuck spoke from the doorway. "Sorry, Mae. I didn't know. Garrison just told her it was a joke, but she's not completely buying it."

Mae smiled at Mrs. Ethelmeyer. "He's trying to pull a fast one on you. He's been doing that all summer. A practical joker, my grandson."

Garrison opened his mouth to speak, but Mae swatted his knee. "Oh you, pulling the leg of our guest." She turned back to Mrs. Ethelmeyer. "I tell you. There was an incident with red dye tablets in the sink. I nearly wet myself."

Garrison stared at Mae. Who was this person?

Mrs. Ethelmeyer apparently wondered that too. "Practical jokes, huh? But there WAS a boy here named Tuck. You said so."

"Mmm-hmm," Mae said, picking up one of the mugs and taking a sip. "Just for a few days. They got along well, doing what boys do."

"And what do boys do?"

Mae shrugged, looking at the floor. "Visiting the cats in the barn, climbing trees, and eating me out of house and home." She fake laughed. "Speaking of, I better start dinner. Are there any more questions you have?"

Mrs. Ethelmeyer's grip on the pen was fierce. "I would like to tour the house."

Mae took another drink. For a moment, Garrison wondered if she would say no. "Sure. I'll take you through right now."

"With Garrison."

"Of course." She stood up. "Come on."

They made an awkward train, especially because Mrs. Ethelmeyer kept looking back at Garrison while Tuck was speaking from behind him. "Just ignore everything. Act normal. She's looking again, trying to judge your reaction. Ignore Paul — don't even look at him. Nope, not at Rebecca either. She'll understand." In the hallways, people jumped aside and stared at them. Mrs. Ethelmeyer didn't acknowledge any of them. Garrison was getting a weird feeling of déjà vu, but he couldn't quite put a finger on it.

Mae led everyone down the main staircase and back to the front door. She held it open. "Well, it was kind of you to visit us, Mrs. Ethelmeyer."

Mrs. Ethelmeyer snapped her black book shut, then looked at them both. She turned to Mae. "I don't need to tell you how bizarre this was, do I?"

Mae said nothing.

"This isn't over." She held out a business card. "I encourage you to reach out to Doctor Browning for an assessment of legal competency."

"That's ridiculous," Mae said with venom. "Please leave my house."

Mrs. Ethelmeyer nodded, placing the card on a small table near the door. She walked over the threshold. Mae barely waited for her heel to clear before slamming the door shut.

Garrison was about to ask what the hell was going on, but she put her finger to her lips. Garrison could see Mrs. Ethelmeyer on the porch, hovering. Mae motioned for him to follow her back down the hall. The moment her back was turned, he grabbed the small card from the table, then followed.

As they entered the kitchen, Mae turned around to face him. "I'm sure you have questions."

Garrison exploded. "Questions?! She couldn't see Tuck. Or Paul. Or Rebecca! Any of them. Why?"

Tuck interjected. "I told you it would come to this." He was stealing a cookie from one of the boxes Mae kept in the top cabinets.

"You are not helping, Tuck." Mae sighed. "This...this isn't easy to say. I haven't told anyone in, well, 30 years, give or take." Her gaze drifted off for a moment.

"Are they ghosts?" Garrison asked. He looked at Tuck. "Are you dead?"

"Do I look dead?"

"Ghosts don't have to look dead."

"How would you know?"

"TUCK!" Mae shouted. "Would you please excuse us for a bit?"

Tuck took two more cookies and left the kitchen in a huff.

"I need more coffee." Mae went to the counter. Garrison turned his palm to read the card Mrs. Ethelmeyer left.

Robert B. Browning
Counselor and School Psychologist
325 W. Main St., Morgansville, WI
R_browning@emailme.com
555-URHELPER

Psychologist. Suddenly, the card morphed into a plastic placard that read, Phil Golderberg, Child Psychologist. Garrison remembered the small yellow room, cheery if not for the smell of toilet bowl cleaner.

Dr. Golderberg was asking Garrison about Arthur. If he saw him today?

Yes.

If he goes to school with Garrison?

No.

If Garrison knows he's made up?

Garrison didn't know how to answer that last one. Arthur came over nearly every day. They pretended the top of the playset slide was a pirate ship and took turns making each other walk the plank. Or they would spy on the neighbors in stealth mode, reporting about suspicious dog-walking and illegal grass-watering.

On the other hand, Garrison knew he was at Dr. Golderberg's because of Arthur. It happened a few weeks before. Garrison was showing Arthur his Lego dragon with moveable claws when his mother called him to the table. "Want to stay for dinner?" Garrison asked him.

Arthur paused, thinking about it.

Garrison never had a friend over for dinner before. He knew his parents would say yes. "Come on. It will be fun," he pushed.

"Okay," Arthur said, shrugging.

Garrison led the way down the hall when he thought of something. "Do you need to ask your mom or something?"

Arthur shook his head.

When they entered the small eat-in kitchen, his father was already sitting at the head of the table. His mother was passing around plates.

"Can Arthur stay for dinner?"

The room got strangely silent. His parents looked at each other.

Slowly, his mother asked, "Who's Arthur?"

"My friend." Garrison gestured to him. Arthur was standing beside him, fiddling with his feet. "Arthur, you want to stay for dinner, right?"

"If that's okay?"

Garrison turned to his mother. She wasn't answering. "Is it?"

"Is it what?"

"Okay that he stays for dinner."

"Sure," his mother said uncertainly. She glanced again at his father. "I'll go get an extra plate."

"No, you won't. Rachel, sit down."

Garrison's mother sat. His father took a deep breath. "I'm ending this now, before it gets a foothold." He turned to Garrison. "Garrison. There is no one there."

"There is! He's right there! Arthur, say something to my dad."

Arthur uttered something unintelligible.

His father scowled.

The fake laugh his mother tried did nothing to lighten the mood. So instead, she said, "Gary, at his age, there's nothing wrong with having an imaginary friend. It's not the same as..."

"He's not imaginary!" Garrison stomped his foot. "He's right next to me."

Arthur sighed. "I think I better go," he said, but Garrison barely noticed.

"Rachel, you may call it an eccentricity, but Garrison is my son. I don't want that to happen to him." He squinted at Garrison. "Listen to me, Garrison. There is no one there."

"There is!"

"Go to your room."

"But that's not fair!"

His father stood and bellowed at him across the table. "GO TO YOUR ROOM."

Garrison's heart was pounding. His father's face had red blotches and his eyes were hard rocks. Garrison ran to his room.

The fighting between his parents started that night. After a week of it, his mother brought him to Dr. Golderberg's office.

Dr. Golderberg explained that imaginary friends were fine, up to a point. He talked about having one himself, a blue cow that could fly. But it was important that Garrison distinguished between what was real and what was not.

Garrison tried. He told Arthur that he wasn't real. At first, Arthur was confused, then angry. Finally, Garrison was forced to shout at him to leave and never come back.

His father spanked him for that one. And yelled at his mother. He seemed to blame her, for some reason. Garrison promised to never speak of Arthur again, but it didn't help. The divorce was final by Christmas that year, almost 7 years ago.

"Garrison!"

Mae's voice was sharp. Sam and Rebecca were standing behind her now. "It's all imaginary, isn't it?" Garrison asked, letting the card fall. "I'm seeing things again."

"What are you talking about?" Mae asked, picking up the card and turning it over to read it.

Garrison couldn't answer. His stomach burned.

Mae put a hand on his shoulder. He looked at her, her eyes gray. Just like his. She spoke firmly, but quietly. "I see them too. Remember?"

Garrison blinked. Maybe he wasn't crazy. Or maybe Mae was? That would explain the townspeople, wouldn't it? The allegations. She saw dead people? Or people who weren't there at all. He felt his chest tighten. It was hard to breathe.

"Just relax," said Rebecca, pushing forward. She put a cold cloth on his head. "Breathe. It will be alright."

CHAPTER 10

Garrison watched Mae. They were sitting across from each other at the kitchen island, while Rebecca made soothing sounds. Mae folded and unfolded her hands a few times. "Garrison," she started. Then stopped. She took a deep breath. "You might find this hard to believe — lord knows I did, but, well, there are other places, realms, I guess. I don't really know what to call them, but they are different realities than our own."

Garrison couldn't help himself. It was too ridiculous. "Are you seriously suggesting there's a multiverse? Like in a Marvel movie?"

"I don't know what that means, but perhaps. The people here all come from a different realm. They have a queen and lord-run fiefdoms and towns. It sounds very medieval, from what Sam and Tuck tell me. This is a place they can cross over into our world. When they do, they can't be seen. Unless someone is very sensitive. Someone like us."

Garrison hugged himself. "Sounds made up," he mumbled.

"I suppose. I learned early on to say I was thinking out loud when I got caught talking to them. Like that day you first arrived. I realized I spoke to Tuck and tried to explain it away. I didn't realize then that you had the sight as well. Not until Tuck told me later, but I didn't believe him. I didn't want to, because it's not easy to live with. I wanted to see for myself. Remember that first breakfast?"

Garrison nodded. "You came to get me and sent me into the dining room."

Mae nodded. "I followed you. My heart sank as I saw you look around at everyone. Still, I told myself if I could keep you away from most of it, then maybe...oh, I don't know." She used her hand to rub her face.

"Why didn't my mom tell me?"

Mae gave him a sad smile. "She can't see them. It was so hard for her, growing up here. If one of them forgot about her and moved something inside the room, she saw it. For a long time, she thought this house was haunted."

"Haunted?"

Mae nodded.

"So they *are* ghosts?"

"I don't think so. There is no record of any of them ever living before. Not in the human world, anyway."

He looked at the floor.

"Lawrence couldn't see them either. He would have been your grandfather." Mae looked away, unfocused.

This was the first time Mae ever mentioned him. Garrison decided to ask the question. It came out as a whisper. "What happened to him? I mean, he died, right?"

"He must have," Mae said slowly, looking down. "He disappeared. Not long after I told him what I just told you."

"What?"

"I was pregnant with your mother. I thought I should be honest with him."

Garrison waited, not sure what to say.

"Lawrence was the only person I ever told about them. When he was declared dead, I swore I would never tell anyone ever again."

"Including Mom?"

Mae nodded. The corners of her mouth turned down at the edges even more.

"Didn't she wonder, though?" Garrison pushed. "Did she hear you talking to them?"

Mae took a deep breath and let it out. "I told her I talked to myself. And I suppose she never knew differently. I tried to be careful. And there weren't very many at first. One or two people a month. More came later. Honestly, the hardest thing to explain was the extra food I made. The guests ate in their rooms, but I had to cook it. She asked me about it once. I said I gave it to neighbors and the soup kitchen. Eventually, I sent her to boarding school. I told her it was to culture her, to get her away from this small-minded town. And it was. And wasn't." Mae paused, then continued. "After taking her first high school psychology class, though, I think she wondered a bit. I remember she asked me questions about mental health. Talked to me about schizophrenia and multiple personality disorders. I knew what she was doing. She even asked me if I saw people who weren't there."

"What did you say?"

"I said no. And I was being honest. Because they ARE there. They even have a name; the Anthropi Avra."

Garrison let that sink in a moment, then made a face. "Maybe you should have told her, anyway. Made her understand."

Mae shook her head. "It changed Lawrence. I couldn't bear to see it do that to Rachel. It's better she doesn't know."

Garrison privately disagreed.

They sat in silence for a bit, absorbed in their own thoughts. Eventually, Mae said, "Garrison. When you read that card for Robert B. Browning," she spat the name, "you said something strange. 'I'm seeing things again.' What did you mean?"

Garrison thought about not telling her. He barely knew her. Not really. Yet, it didn't seem fair somehow. She shared so much with him. Plus, the kitchen was warm and full of a savory smell. Mae must have something in the slow cookers. Garrison decided to tell her the truth. "When I was younger, I had an imaginary friend. Well, maybe it wasn't imaginary. I don't know. Mom took me to a psychologist and everything. It's why Mom and Dad...broke up."

Mae sighed. "It probably was one of them. But even if it wasn't, the divorce wasn't your fault. You know that, right?"

Garrison said nothing.

"I remember when she brought him to meet me." Mae looked like her mouth tasted of lemons. "They stayed the night. I suppose he hoped for a snack or more dessert, because he came down into the kitchen late that night. After we all said goodnight. Well, I was talking to Sam and another man staying here — you need to understand; I thought it was safe — but he heard and made a strangled gasp. I whirled around and saw him, white as a ghost. He shook his head and ran. I followed, trying to come up with a plausible explanation. He was already back in their room with the door locked and yelling at Rachel. 'And there she was. Talking to herself,' he said."

"I told you she does that," Rachel said. "She likes to think out loud."

"No! This was an entire conversation. As though someone was answering her. A ghost. Or just thin air. Something in her own head. I don't know, but she's certifiable."

"Gary, you're overreacting! She's just eccentric, not crazy. If she was schizophrenic or something, she wouldn't be able to manage this house and the farm all on her own. She does just fine, even makes extra food each day to take to the neighbors and the homeless. She's good. You were probably half asleep. Come back to bed."

Mae smiled a sad smile. I don't think your father ever really forgot about that. They left early the next morning. And he never visited again, even though it hurt your mother's feelings. No compassion, even then. Don't you worry about him."

Garrison didn't know what to say. He felt a bit relieved, and also guilty.

Tuck came into the kitchen, interrupting. "I'm starving. When's dinner?"

Mae checked her watch. "Oh, Lord." She popped up and started moving around the kitchen, lifting lids, tasting.

Tuck leaned towards him and whispered, "Want to come to see Carly tonight?"

Garrison glanced at Mae. Her back was to them. "Mmm," he said in confirmation. While he wasn't sure what was true or what was going on, he knew one thing. Tuck knew more than he was telling. Maybe the girl did too.

"Better meet me there at 6:30 since dinner is so late."

Garrison nodded.

CHAPTER 11

Carly stared at the note for the thousandth time.

KEEP YOUR MOUTH SHUT

Every time she read it, she got a chill up her spine. The handwriting, thick black capitals, told her little. Only that the person was vehement. The phrasing was a bit more to go on. Aggressive. The note came just after the two boys brought her lunch, slipped under her door, maybe 20 minutes later. She hadn't been paying attention to the time before it came.

She read the note again, hoping this time it would spark a memory. What was she supposed to keep her mouth shut about? What did she know?

There was a knock at her door.

"Just a minute," she called. She shoved the note between her mattress and box spring. She was just straightening the blanket cover when she said, "Enter."

She winced at the word. Why did she keep saying that?

The door swung open to reveal the boys. Now that she saw them again, she recalled their names, Tuck and Garrison. She tried not to stare at Garrison. There was something about him, something that nagged at the part of her mind that was blocked. He barely seemed to notice her today, though.

"Okay, so you don't think you're a ghost, but you might be." Garrison was saying to Tuck, who put her tray of food on the dresser. "Can you walk through walls?"

Tuck sighed. "No. I can't."

Garrison turned towards her. "What about you? Do your bruises come back each day? Maybe you died out there, and don't realize it."

Carly took a step backwards. "What's going on?"

Tuck answered. "Garrison just found out he can see us when most humans can't."

"Not most, ANY!" Garrison corrected.

Carly met Garrison's eyes. "You didn't know? Didn't see anyone when you were little? I heard they do. Our children are drawn to them sometimes, crossing over at random. One moment, they are in our world and the next—" she snapped her fingers.

Garrison looked away, but Tuck was suddenly alert. "THEY do? Our children are drawn to them?"

His eyes were narrow, accusing. Carly shook her head. "I don't know what I meant by that," she mumbled. "It was something I heard."

"From whom?"

Carly pulled on the collar of her dress. "Listen, I don't remember."

In truth, there was something coming back to her. A blonde boy with pale blue eyes. He was throwing grapes up and catching them in his mouth while he talked to her. She remembered him saying, "He keeps paying the CARBs to be informants."

"The CARBs?" she asked him.

The boy looked at her. His startling blue eyes were almost bored. "The Child and Adolescent Retrieval Brigade. Kids cross over sometimes, without meaning to. Especially when a silver-eyed child is around. The CARBs go get them if they can't get back on their own. He's hoping one of them sees the silver-eyed one. Then he can get to them before they grow up and beat him."

Carly almost laughed. "But who could beat him?"

He threw another grape in his mouth. "The Fotismeno," he said around it. "Remember what the fortune teller said?"

She did. The boy snuck her out of the house to visit the old woman with him. She was heavily wrinkled and spoke in a low voice as she walked through her greenhouse, looking at the plants. "I see the bloom of shadow as a time of action nears," she said, snipping a blood red rose from its stem. She spun to face a white-flowering plant growing up the wall, as though it called out. "Plaiting vines of fate mean the ring will soon appear." Another hard snip.

Finally, she cocked her head as though listening. "Victory!" she shouted. She pulled a sprout from a small pot on the window. "For you." She turned to the boy with blue eyes. "Sune. It's planted with a seed of fear." She handed him the offerings. "A fortune for your father."

Carly snickered. "Yes. But when he told the story at dinner that night, he called her a crazy old lady."

The boy looked away. "She's my great aunt."

Carly immediately felt uncomfortable. "I'm sorry, Sune. I didn't know."

The boy shrugged, but she could tell he felt wounded. She focused on the fortune instead. "Even so, doesn't that mean his plan will work? I mean, she said 'the bloom of darkness' and 'Victory.'"

"Maybe. But this war is drawing too much attention. And that ring he's after, it's the Fotismeno's. They were silver-eyed ones. Remember?"

Carly and Sune both turned at a knock on the door. "That will be my maid," she said. "You better go."

Sune nodded, climbing over to the window. "See you tonight, my princess." His smile was dazzling. They were just friends, but that smile made her stomach do flips. And he knew it. She pulled the drapes over him and called towards the door, "Enter."

The memory of the maid coming in with a tray faded as Carly came back to the present. Garrison and Tuck were staring at her. Had she said anything? She wrapped her arms around her chest. "What is it?" she asked them.

Garrison shook his head. "You went all quiet. Do your bruises come back or not?"

"No. We're not ghosts, okay?"

"Then why am I the only one who can see you?"

"Because you're a silver-eyed one. Just get over it."

There was a frosty silence in the room. Carly looked over at Tuck. His mouth was open. "What did you call him?"

Carly panicked. "I don't know. Look at him. He has silver-gray eyes. I just figured...you know...so does his grandmother."

Tuck looked thoughtful. Carly thought she saw a way out of this. "You know how people say blue-eyed people can see better in the dark? Well, I figured it stood to reason that sil—" she interrupted herself, "gray-eyed people can see, well, us. That's all. Why does it mean something?" She faced Tuck, making her eyes as wide as possible.

Tuck's tense shoulders eased a bit, but he still looked suspicious. She turned to Garrison and smiled. "Your family must be really special to have one of the protected places."

"Okay, that's enough," Tuck called into the room.

Garrison just stared at her.

What had she said? She was trying to give him a compliment.

"Come on, Garrison, let's go."

Tuck had to physically push Garrison towards the door, but he continued to argue. "No. No, what do you mean? What are protected places?"

Carly bit her lip, but didn't answer.

"Seriously, Tuck. What the heck is going on?"

"Later," Tuck said through clenched teeth. He opened the door.

Standing in the hall was a man. Carly felt the blood suddenly drain from her face. Her limbs got weak.

"Oh, hi, boys. I thought I heard voices coming from the girl's room." He looked directly into Carly's eyes. "Evening, Miss."

She gulped, trying to breathe. She knew him.

"Hi, Paul," Tuck said with a smile. "We were just delivering dinner."

"Very good," the man said. He nodded at them and headed down the hall. Carly didn't dare lean out to watch, but she heard a door open and close. He must be staying here as well. She was almost sure he sent the note.

"Lord, I hope he doesn't tell Mae you were in there too," Tuck muttered, stepping out into the hall. "She might actually kill me." He closed the door.

Carly barely noticed because she was too busy thinking about the man. Paul is what Tuck called him. She knew him as something else, someone Sune pointed out months ago. He was leaving the estate. "See him," Sune said. "My dad gave him a mission. He has a talent for uncovering secrets. It's interesting, considering you said my dad mocked my great-aunt's talent."

Had the man been here all that time? What was the secret?

Carly went to the door of her blue bedroom and tried the knob. Locked. She wasn't sure if that made her feel safe or trapped. Was she supposed to be here? Did she have a mission she couldn't remember? Or was there something else? She put her head in her hands. She didn't know.

CHAPTER 12

Tuck took Garrison outside, to the very edge of the property. For a moment, he thought they were going to go into the forest together, breaking another of Mae's rules, but Tuck stopped near a metal pole with a box on top. Garrison looked closer. The base was elaborate, full of embossed vines and leaves climbing up the pole and around the box at the top. There was a horizontal slit near the top of the box, and a word. He traced it with his finger. MAIL. "What is this?" he asked

Tuck barely glanced at it. "A mailbox."

Garrison glared at him. "Right. But what is it doing here? Instead of at the road?"

Tuck shrugged. He picked up a stone from the ground and threw it at a dead tree a few yards away. "Bet you can't hit that hollowed out hole in the center."

Garrison turned his back on the antique mailbox and glanced at the tree before turning back to Tuck. "I don't care about the hollow. Or the mailbox, really. I want to know what a protected place is? What's so special about this house? What the heck are any of you even doing here? I mean, if you are even real."

Tuck picked up another rock. This one was red quartz, and it glinted in the setting sun as Tuck turned it this way and that. "I don't think I'm supposed to tell you."

Garrison saw the way his mouth twitched as he said the words. Tuck's rebellious streak was showing. "But you will, right?" Garrison asked, pushing.

Tuck threw the red stone. It sailed right into the hollow, making a soft thud. "You could say we are here because of an ancient pact."

"We, as in the Anthropi Avra?"

"Mmm. There's a legend that someone from our side, a man, found a way through the barrier between our worlds. Not only did he get through to yours, but he could excite certain emotions in humans, almost like he could control their actions. He called himself the God of Darkness and brought others over to feed on the raw, primal emotions he inspired — fear, aggression, suspicion. It created chaos. And war." Tuck bent to pick up another rock and threw it. Garrison had to squint to see it in the darkening air. It bounced off the bark a little to the left of the hole. Tuck went on. "But our worlds are connected. The man's rise brought unrest to our cities as well. It was a grisly age in our history. Until the queen gained power."

"Mae mentioned you have a queen."

It was hard to tell, but it looked like Tuck grimaced. "She's the head of the current reigning royal family. Vowing to fight back, to regain balance for our world, she formed an alliance with the special group of humans able to see us.

Well, see us and not decide they were insane." He gave Garrison a look.

Garrison ignored it.

"Anyway, together, they somehow beat the man and brought peace to the world."

Garrison cocked an eyebrow. "That's it? That's the end of the story?"

"It is a legend. They aren't usually brimming with details."

"But how? If he could control humans, how were there any who could fight against him?"

Tuck turned to him. "He couldn't control humans. None of us can. It's just that we can manipulate certain unseen energies around you. It might fuel an emotion or a certain outcome."

"What the heck does that mean? You can manipulate me?"

"No. And maybe yes."

Garrison didn't like the tone of Tuck's voice. It was too playful. "Seriously. You need to explain that."

Tuck crossed his arms. "Remember that gang of boys in town? The ones with the skateboards?"

Garrison gave an involuntary shutter. "Yeah."

"Do you remember how they tripped on those loose stones?"

"Yeah."

Tuck pointed to himself. "You're welcome."

Garrison still didn't understand. "Wait. That was you?"

"Well, it wasn't a coincidence," Tuck snapped. Garrison's lack of understanding seemed to annoy him. "Listen. I'm an effectus," he said. "So, I can manipulate the energy around an event or group of people. I make whatever they are planning go all wrong."

Garrison didn't think the pride in Tuck's voice was warranted. "You make plans go wrong...so, like a jinx or something?"

"Jinx, curse, karma, comeuppance — it depends on your point of view."

Garrison pressed his palms to his eyes. "So you and everyone else here has some kind of jinx power over humans?"

"Noooo," Tuck dragged out the word. "*I* have the so-called jinx power. Other people have other abilities. Mae only helps the benevolent ones. Or tries to anyway."

"Uh, what does benevolent mean?"

Tuck rolled his eyes. "Seriously. What is wrong with human schools? It means kind, well-intentioned. Stuff like compassion, unity, reasoning. The queen's lackeys."

It didn't sound like a compliment. "The queen's one of the good guys, though, right? I mean, if that man from your story was evil, she's good?"

Tuck bent down, looking for another stone.

"Tuck? Is she good?"

"I guess."

"What does that mean?"

Tuck stood with a handful and looked at the tree. "It means that—" He never got to finish because someone called their names. It was Sam, walking towards them. He didn't look happy.

"What's wrong?" Tuck asked.

"There's a message for you."

"From who?"

"Whom," Sam corrected, then he winced. It felt like an apology. "It's from…" he glanced at Garrison, then continued, "her majesty. You are to leave immediately."

"You're kidding?"

"I wish I were."

"Why? She hasn't called me back in years."

"Would you like me to—"

"NO!" Tuck shouted. "There's nothing you can do." He threw his handful of rocks to the ground so hard they bounced, making dozens of tiny thuds. He ran towards the house.

"Wait," Garrison called after him. "Where are you going?"

"None of your beeswax," Tuck called back.

Garrison blinked in surprise.

Sam put a hand on Garrison's shoulder. "Don't mind him. He's upset."

"But he's leaving?"

Sam's eyes softened. "Yes. "

"You said her majesty. Is that, like, your queen?"

Sam glanced after Tuck. Garrison wondered if he was angry about what Tuck told him. If Sam was, he didn't sound it. "Yes. It is the queen. Tuck is her official messenger."

"So, he just has to go?" What Garrison couldn't say was that he didn't want Tuck to go. Tuck was the only one he could talk to. Tuck couldn't just leave.

"It's not easy being special," Sam said, as though that answered his question. "But you should know that." He squeezed Garrison's shoulder, then let go. His head was bent low as he walked away.

It was too hard to process all this information. A different world, manipulatable energy, a dark god and a possibly not good queen. It was all so strange. Like a video game. And what Sam said about being special. Why was Tuck special? Why was Garrison? He looked out at the dark trees. Was that a light in the darkness? A tall shape, like a house? A sudden breeze picked up, making the branches of the tree Tuck was throwing stones at wave menacingly. Garrison took a step backward. He looked again, but there were just more trees. He decided it was time to go back inside.

CHAPTER 13

The next morning, Garrison sat at the kitchen counter. He stared out the side door. A clock somewhere ticked the seconds as they passed. He wondered if Tuck would come back today.

Someone cleared their throat behind him.

Garrison turned to see Mae holding a tray. "What will you be doing today?" she asked.

He shrugged. With Tuck gone, it felt like his first day here all over again. He half-expected Mae to tell him to go back to his room.

"Well. I, um..." Mae stuttered and then started again. "I could use some help."

Garrison was speechless.

"You could burn the paper trash," she said. "Maybe even..." she looked down at the tray she was holding, "...take this to Carly's room."

Garrison swallowed hard at the name. His heart began pumping blood to his face. He desperately tried to keep his face expressionless. "Sure. I don't mind helping."

Mae narrowed her eyes at him, just a little. Could she hear his heart beating? Was she rethinking letting him upstairs?

"She's in room 12, upstairs. You remember?"

He nodded as he stood and headed towards her. He reached for the tray. She didn't let go. He looked into her eyes.

"Just be careful."

"I won't spill. I've got it."

Mae shook her head. "That's not what...never mind."

Garrison was confused. She couldn't mean to be careful of Carly? What could she possibly do to him? Then he remembered what Tuck told him last night. Maybe the girl could make him scared. Or fall madly in love. He suddenly wasn't sure he wanted to take the breakfast tray. But Mae let go then, and Garrison felt the full weight in his hands. He steadied the tray, and himself, and nodded again. He would be careful.

Turning, he climbed up the narrow back stairs to the second floor. He felt like Mae was watching him, but he decided not to turn around and check.

On the second floor, he headed straight to Carly's door. He balanced the tray in one hand and knocked.

"Enter."

Garrison turned the knob, but the door was locked. Tuck always had a key, but he didn't have it. He was about to turn back when he spotted the key on the tray. Mae must have put it there. He picked it up and unlocked the door. It swung open with only a slight nudge.

Carly was standing by the window. She watched him enter the room.

"Hi," he said. This was so much easier without Tuck around.

"Hello."

"Um...I brought you breakfast."

She nodded and waved to the dresser. Garrison put down the tray and straightened up. He cleared his throat.

He noticed Carly was wearing a different dress today. This one was blue with flowers on it.

Carly crossed her arms over her chest.

He cleared his throat again. "Can I ask you something?"

"Isn't that what you're doing?"

He took that as a yes. "What can you do?"

"Pardon?"

"Like, what, um...energy can you manipulate?"

Carly blinked at him. Then she looked at the floor with a furrowed brow. "That sounds familiar, but I don't think I can."

Garrison didn't know why, but he felt better. "You can't manipulate anything?"

Carly shook her head. "I don't think so. Nothing in the human world, anyway."

Garrison almost smiled, but caught himself. She didn't look happy. "Does that bother you?"

"No. That doesn't. Not being able to remember bothers me. Being cooped up in this room all day, every day, bothers me."

"Oh. I didn't realize you were—"

"A prisoner?"

He stared at her.

She turned her gaze to the floor. "Sorry," she muttered.

Garrison looked at the floor too. "I could ask if you could leave the room. I mean, sometimes, or whatever. I don't know."

She studied him and the corners of her eyes softened. "That would be very nice. Thank you."

He nodded. He wasn't ready to leave yet, but he didn't know what more to say.

"Is there something else?" Carly asked.

He shook his head. "No. No. It's just my friend Tuck left, and I don't know what to do." He couldn't believe he said that. He gave himself a mental facepalm.

She let her arms drop to her sides. "I saw him leave."

"You did?"

She nodded. "From the window."

Garrison glanced at her window. She had a view of the yard and forest, not the front of the house. How did Tuck leave?

"Why did he have to go?" she asked.

Still distracted, Garrison answered, "Your queen wanted him to come. She wants him to carry a message or something."

"He's the queen's messenger?" she asked, wide-eyed.

Garrison shrugged. "I guess. Why? What does that mean?"

Carly looked away. "Nothing, really. I guess I'm just surprised."

"Why? Because he's so young?"

She laughed. "No. Because that means he's a Shamington."

"A what?"

She moved to her desk. "One of the royal families. A few decades ago, they tried to start a rebellion."

Garrison felt his jaw drop. "A rebellion?"

She nodded, sitting in her desk chair. "Mm-hm. To overthrow the queen. It failed, obviously. And now all the Shamingtons are either imprisoned or forced to serve her majesty."

Garrison let that soak into his head. *Forced to serve.* Could that be why Tuck didn't consider the queen good?

"He didn't tell you." It was more of a statement than a question.

"No," Garrison said anyway. He looked at Carly, at her green eyes. They seemed sad, as though she knew how much it hurt that Tuck hadn't confided in him.

"I'm sorry," she said.

Garrison just nodded. He wanted to think. "I better go."

"Of course."

He backed out of the door and closed it. His hand was on the knob. Should he leave it unlocked for her?

"Aren't you forgetting something?" It was Carly's voice.

He opened the door an inch. She held the key up. He must have left it on the tray. She smiled at him.

A warm feeling bubbled in his chest. She had the chance to keep the key. To let herself out of the room, a place she said she was sick of being in. Yet, she didn't. He liked that about her. He smiled back and took the key. "See you later," he said.

She nodded.

This time, he closed and locked the door.

CHAPTER 14

Garrison didn't immediately go to find Mae. He knew she would be in the yard, doing chores now, so he went to his bedroom to think. Tuck was part of a royal family. Was he a prince? Garrison felt that was a disturbing thought. He glanced over at Tuck's empty bed. It seemed like it was taking over the entire room, making everything feel empty. He wondered where Tuck was now. Kneeling in front of some evil queen, forced to go on dangerous missions. Would he ever come back? The images definitely felt like scenes from a video game, so Garrison hoped he was just being dramatic. Something he never hoped before.

He wondered if Tuck's grandfather was still alive, the one that taught him the card tricks. Was he in prison? What about Tuck's mom and dad? He never mentioned them. Were they in prison, too? Or did they die in the rebellion?

It was impossible to know. Maybe because Tuck was a kid, he was spared from jail. Although being a servant was probably not much better. Tuck seemed pretty angry when he left.

At 11:30, Garrison pushed himself off the bed and went to the dining room. It wasn't very crowded. Mae was just putting down a bowl of potato salad on the sideboard next to a plate of sandwiches. Garrison went up to her.

"Can I talk to you?" he asked.

She furrowed her brow. "What about?"

Garrison looked around. There were two men at a table, but they were talking to each other. He turned back to Mae. "It's about Carly. Is she...well, a prisoner?"

Mae shook her head. "No, of course not."

"But she's locked in her room and never allowed out."

Mae winced at his words.

Garrison decided that was a good sign. "Could she leave for a short time, maybe? Say a walk around the yard?"

Mae frowned at him.

He put up his hands. "Hear me out. The fresh air would be good for her memory. And I'd stay with her the entire time. Then she can go right back and be locked in."

Mae raised an eyebrow. "Did she ask to leave her room?"

"No. She just seemed frustrated with being stuck in it all the time."

Mae nodded. "I can't blame her. It's just that—"

"We don't know who did that to her?" Garrison asked.

"That too."

Garrison felt his brow grow furrowed, but Mae spoke before he could ask his question. "Alright. A short walk after lunch. Around the yard. But Garrison, no matter what she does or says, promise me you'll stay on the property. No matter what. Promise?"

Garrison promised.

"Good," Mae said with a deep breath. "Now come on. I have her lunch ready. You can go tell her the good news with her tray."

Garrison smiled, grabbing a sandwich, and followed her into the kitchen.

About a half hour later, after Garrison ensured Carly ate ALL her lunch, they went outside. Carly looked around as they walked through the halls, as though she was worried about being caught.

"I told you. I asked her," Garrison said, trying to reassure her.

She just shook her head.

Garrison took her out the kitchen door, into the side yard. It was his preferred door, because the porch wasn't really large enough for lounging. There wouldn't be anyone there to stare at them. As soon as Carly was outside, she looked up at the sky. It was pale blue without a single cloud.

Garrison's attention was caught by how the sun made her hair glow copper. It was cliche, but it was the exact color of a new penny.

"It's so nice to be outside," Carly said. "Thank you again for talking to your grandma."

He reached up to rub his cheek, trying to hide the sudden heat there. "It was no problem. Really."

She smiled at him.

They walked along the driveway towards the road, then looped back along the other side where it went around some trees and flowers. "So, do you come here often to visit your grandmother?"

Garrison shook his head. "No. This is actually the first time I've been here."

"Really? That seems strange."

"I suppose." Garrison didn't feel like going into all that right now. "Um, how old are you?"

Carly looked at the tree line. "I don't know."

"Sorry. I forgot." He rubbed the back of his head. "I'm 14, going to be 15 this year. You're probably that old, too." It sounded a bit too hopeful.

They were just coming up to the barn. Garrison thought he could change the subject. Maybe show Carly Lawrence's workshop. But a noise made him stop. "What was that?" he asked.

Carly stopped too, cocking her head to the side. "It sounds like an animal. One that's in trouble." She started moving towards the barn's long wall.

Garrison knew this area. It was where Mae threw vegetable skins, eggshells, and other food trash. The refuse was contained by a rectangular pen divided into three sections with boards nailed across the front. He and Tuck usually avoided it due to the smell.

The sound came again from one of the compartments. "Meeeew."

Carly put a foot on the bottom board of the middle section and hoisted herself up to see inside. Garrison joined her. At first, he just saw clumpy-looking dirt, flecked with grass clippings and decaying leftovers, but then something moved. In the very corner was a small creature with blue eyes.

"Mew," it said, showing needle-like teeth.

"Oh my word," cried Carly. "It's a kitten. It must have gotten stuck in here." She stretched her hand down and wiggled her fingers at it. "Come on. Come on," she coaxed. She mimed coming towards her.

The kitten didn't come.

"There's something wrong." She turned towards Garrison. Her eyes were huge and wet and intensely green. "Maybe she's hurt. We have to help her!"

He looked at Carly's bare legs under her dress and sighed. There was no way he could ask her to climb into a garbage pile. He wished he were here with Tuck, who always wore black.

"Meeeew," the kitten wailed.

Garrison climbed onto the second board and swung his leg up over the last two. He sat on the top as he got his other leg up and over. He dangled them for a moment, trying not to breathe in the smell, and then dropped.

"Be careful." He heard Carly say the moment he pushed off. He smiled to himself as he landed. The compost gave way beneath him and he lurched sideways. He flung out his hand to catch himself, and it sank into a pile of old potato peelings. "Gross!" He yanked his hand back quickly. "Wow. It's hot."

"Hot?"

"Yeah. Like really hot." Garrison looked around for the kitten. It was still there, half-buried in one corner. Its mouth was open like it was panting. He bent his knees, trying to maintain his balance on the constantly shifting ground. He took a step towards the kitten, talking in a soothing tone. "It's okay. Did you crawl in here and get stuck? I won't hurt you. Let me take you back to your mom."

The kitten didn't resist as his fingers wrapped around it. He pulled it close to his chest, and it made the same vibrating noise as a video game controller. He laughed at the unexpected sensation.

"What's humorous?"

"Nothing," said Garrison, walking back to her. "It's just...I think it's purring."

"Here, hand it over." Carly reached out and Garrison transferred the tiny bundle to her. Then he climbed up the inside of the bin and jumped back to the ground.

Carly was inspecting the kitten when he looked up. It certainly was filthy. Carly brushed some of the dirt and peelings off. "I can feel her ribs," she said. She bit her lip.

"Let's get it back to its mom," Garrison said. "They're usually in the barn, in one of the stalls." He led the way, Carly cradling the purring kitten behind him.

The mama cat Garrison remembered from one of his first days here was resting on a hay bale. She was outside the stall door, which was lucky since Garrison remembered the horrendous noise it made when he opened it. As he watched her licking her paw, a small black fuzz ball darted out and jumped at her throat. The mama cat curled it into her stomach and Garrison realized it was another of the kittens.

"Perfect," Carly said beside him. She stepped forward, putting the kitten down a foot from the mama cat. It stood stiffly, staring at its mother. The mother flipped herself upright, knocking the other kitten to the ground, and stared back.

"What's wrong?" Carly asked.

Garrison wasn't sure if she was asking him or the cats. Either way, there was no answer. Eventually, the mama cat jumped lightly off the hay. She didn't go up to her dirty baby, but she raised her nose towards it. Her whiskers twitched. Then she laid her ears back flat, hissing.

Garrison was horrified. "What's wrong with you?" he yelled. The mama cat jumped at his voice, or maybe his tone. She darted through the stall door and disappeared.

Carly scooped the dirty kitten back up. "The other ones look plump and clean."

"Yeah," Garrison agreed, trying to figure out why it bothered him so much that the mama cat hissed. "Maybe she just needs a bath. Maybe the mom didn't like the smell."

"I don't think that's it." Carly's voice sounded like a sob. "What if she's been abandoned?"

Garrison felt a lump in his throat. That's exactly what he was trying not to think.

"I just...I just...she can't DIE!" Carly wailed. "She's so small. So helpless." Carly rubbed her face in the kitten's horrible fur and Garrison tried not to cringe. "Garrison!"

It was the first time she had said his name. It sounded good coming from her lips. He stared at them, slightly open, with just a bit of white teeth between. He looked away, shaking himself.

"What are we gonna to do?" She looked at him. To him. Her eyes were so large, her skin so smooth. He knew he was done for. "We're going to take care of her," he said.

Carly's cheeks turned pink. "We are?"

He nodded.

She smiled.

He wanted to do everything he could to keep her smiling.

They walked back to the house.

"When we get there, you wash her in the sink," Carly said. "I need to change my clothes."

Garrison agreed.

They entered the kitchen, and Carly pushed the kitten into his hands. He nearly gagged when the smell reached his nose. It was disgustingly sweet and pungent. He wondered if the kitten itself was decaying. Then he noticed Carly's hand on top of his. His heart did somersaults. Was she going to kiss him on the cheek? He stared at her, willing her to. Her eyes were pools of green, vivid in her pale pink face. Sprinkled with just a few rust-colored freckles. So pretty, he thought.

Carly let go and ran towards the back stairs.

He watched her. She could run up those stairs and then back down the other staircase and out the front door. He wouldn't even know until he visited her room later. She could be long gone before Mae found out. Yet, he knew she wouldn't. He could feel it.

CHAPTER 15

Garrison was elbow deep in suds when Mae walked into the kitchen a few minutes later. She walked over to the sink. "What are you doing?"

Before Garrison could reply, she leaned over. The kitten looked up at her with huge eyes and let out a sorrowful, "Meeeew."

"No. No. No. No. No cats in the house."

"But the mom abandoned her. She'll die."

Mae studied him. "Where's Carly?" she asked.

"In her room."

"Locked in, I'm assuming?"

Garrison nodded. Panic that she ran away exploded inside his head, but he splashed it with positive thoughts. She would be there. After all, she gave him the key earlier and didn't make a single move to leave the grounds on their walk.

Mae's eyes drifted back to the kitten. They softened. He could see it happen, just at the corners. She sighed.

Garrison pushed. "You know Mom's allergic, so I've never been able to have a cat. I've always wanted one."

It wasn't strictly true, but Mae didn't know that.

Mae came over and stroked the now clean, if wet, gray striped fur. The kitten looked at her with its bright blue eyes. "That is quite possibly the most pitiful creature I've ever seen."

Garrison held his breath. There was a noise upstairs, a creak. Please don't make it be Carly, Garrison thought. Then Mae would know I lied.

"It's a big responsibility, having a cat," Mae said.

Garrison focused back on her. "I know. But I'm good at responsibility, just ask my mom. I keep my room clean, mostly. Make my bed. I even cook my own meals when she's at work, and pack one for her, too. "

There it was again, the softening of the eyes, right when he mentioned his mom.

"Alright," Mae said. "But you have to clean up all that water you've spilled on the floor."

Garrison smiled and nodded.

A few minutes later, the kitten was on the counter with a small bowl of milk. Garrison wondered what was taking Carly so long. But even worse, the kitten wouldn't drink. She just stared at Garrison. "Meeeh."

Mae came back into the kitchen and thrust some papers at him.

"What are these?"

"Information about nursing that kitten back to health," said Mae. "Apparently, they can't drink cow's milk. It will starve them to death."

Garrison was appalled.

"I have some evaporated milk around here somewhere. I'll make one of the homemade formula recipes it gives. However, I suggest you read the rest of that article if you want the kitten to have a chance."

Garrison looked down. It was an article printed from the internet titled, *Everything You Need To Know About Raising An Abandoned Kitten.* "So there is internet here?"

Mae was pulling out a pot. "What now?"

Garrison decided it wasn't the time. "Nothing."

While the kitten formula recipe simmered on the stove, Mae brought over a straw. "We don't have a bottle, but it doesn't look like she's strong enough to eat on her own. This will have to do for now."

Garrison cleared his throat. He tried not to sound ungrateful when he asked, "How does a straw help?"

Mae sighed. "Like this." She dipped the straw into the milk on the table. She put her finger on the open top of the straw and lifted it out. When she adjusted her finger to let in a bit of air, a bit of milk dribbled out the bottom.

"Wow," Garrison breathed.

"Mmmm," Mae said. Her cheeks got a blotchy red color and she turned back to the stove. She stirred the formula a few more times and removed it. "We have to let that cool for a bit."

Garrison nodded. He turned back to the article. He skimmed most of it. There was a lot of text. As he started the second page, he frowned. "What does it mean by, 'If neonatal, stimulate their back end until they defecate'?"

Mae looked like she sucked on a lemon. "It means that if they are less than a month old, that you have to rub their private parts until they go to the bathroom."

"You aren't serious."

Now the sour face broke into a smile. "You wanted a kitten," Mae said.

CHAPTER 16

When the door opened, Carly turned around, expecting it to be Garrison with the kitten. It wasn't.

It was Paul.

Or the man they all called Paul. She still couldn't remember his name. Her memory was funny that way. Some things came back easily, when she wasn't trying to remember too hard. Others stubbornly stayed blocked.

"Oh. Um. Hi," she ventured.

"Don't oh, um, hi me. You're making a mess of things." He stepped towards her, towering above her.

She leaned back, trying to get away from him.

"What are you playing at?"

"What do you mean?"

"Amnesia?"

"I...I..."

"You remember plenty. And told it to our enemies." He did a high-pitched voice. "The army is taking over villages and farms. This man with a stag's head hurt me." He curled his lip. "You make me sick," he said in his normal voice. "And what about telling them you're betrothed to him, little princess? Why didn't you mention that?"

Glass shattered in Carly's mind. She knew the tattoo meant something. It was his royal house crest. It meant she was his — under his protection.

She put her hand to her temple and staggered as memories flooded back, clicking into place with her feelings. He was powerful, rich. She was glad to be part of his household. She and her mother had their own wing and servants. They were cut off from all his other doings. Except her mother, who arranged this marriage between her and the older man with the stag features. In exchange for protection. Her mother was special; she was special. Their blood, freely given...was...was...the rest didn't come. She looked up at Paul. "Was what?"

"I don't know what you're playing at. But I have a mission here. I'm close. I can feel the itch in my skin. It means I'm on the right path. And if you compromise me, I will tell everyone your secret."

"No!"

"They'll brand you a traitor and throw you out. Right back to him. Considering what he did to you last time, I wonder what will happen when he gets you back."

Carly turned away from Paul, bent over with the weight of her fear. She suddenly remembered Devose ordering her to come to the great hall for dinner that night. The same day as her mother's funeral. Over hot food, he explained about their marriage. She knew about it. That when she was grown, she would marry him. When he sent a messenger for a priest, she panicked. She told him no. There was such vehemence in the word that all the guests at the table stopped eating.

He stared at her. "No?"

She squared her shoulders. "No," she said defiantly.

His nostrils flared. He snapped his fingers and everyone at the table stood and left, even those who hadn't finished their plates. She stood too, but the guards closed in around her. They grabbed her.

He came to stand before her.

"I thought it would be when I was an adult," she cried.

"Who do you think you are?" he said, his voice wild, full of rage. "No. You are nothing. Get to decide nothing. NO? NO? NO!" He seemed to get more upset with each uttering of the word.

He turned to her and shouted in a language she didn't understand. He slapped her across her face. There were more punches right after, but not from him. The guards. So many that her body felt hot and fiery all over.

At some point, she must have blacked out, because she didn't remember any more until someone gently pushed at her shoulder. She groaned.

"Carly? Carly!" It was Sune's voice, and he sounded frantic. Yet, he was never frantic. He walked around life calm, calculating, always bored. But at this moment, he was afraid. That made her open her eyes.

"Carly," he said again. She could see relief in his eyes. "You have to change."

"I don't want to," she whispered. "I hurt."

Sune looked over his shoulder. "I can't carry you like this. Change! Then I can get you out of here."

"But I have nowhere to go."

"I know of somewhere safe. One of the protected places. It's not far. Come on, Carly. Change."

Suddenly, she was looking up at Sune. He was a giant. He looked strange too, with light surrounding him. The colors...they were off.

He picked her up and cradled her to his chest. He must have been running, because she felt jostled. Pain exploded in every nerve. She closed her eyes and let herself fall into a place between waking and sleeping. Then he roused her.

"Okay. We're here. See that?"

He held her up, and in the distance, she saw a large white house. There were many strange colors around it. Colors she didn't have names for.

"Fly there. Don't stop. Fly right to the door."

"I can't," she said. But the words weren't words when they left her mouth. Instead, they were a chirp. Was she a bird?

"Fly, Carly." He threw her upwards, just like he did dozens of times before. It was a game they used to play. She had no choice. She stretched out her wings and caught the air. A few painful flaps and she was high enough to soar towards the house. Sune whispered something, but she couldn't make it out.

She was nearly at the house when something pushed against her. It was something she couldn't see, but it hurt deep inside. Her muscles spasmed, but she was carried forward with momentum and fell. She reached out her wings again, but they were arms now. She hit the ground and everything went black. That was how she got here, to the Wagon Wheel farm. As a bird.

Carly's body was shaking, but not from her sudden rush of memory. Paul had his hands around her upper arms and was rocking her violently. "Listen up, little princess. Stay out of my way. Don't tell them another thing, not even a small thing. Or else."

She didn't even finish nodding before he was gone, closing the door firmly behind him. Staggering over to her bed, she lay, staring at the wall. How could this be? She was engaged to Devose? She lived with him? Was she evil? No. She couldn't be. Could she? She certainly didn't want to go back. Not to Devose. She couldn't afford to let anything else slip.

***

She was staring out the window, promising herself over and over that she wouldn't tell Garrison anything, when the knock at her door came. For a moment, she worried it was Paul, back again. But he hadn't knocked. She wiped her eyes quickly.

The person at the door didn't wait for her to say anything. They pushed it in slowly. Carly held her breath.

It was Garrison.

She smiled in relief, which, for some reason, made him stop. He looked at the floor as his cheeks went red and blotchy. Did he like her? That made her smile more.

She noticed the kitten in his arms, and she made a happy cry. Tears sprang to her eyes again. But good ones. Which also made her remember the bad ones. So she cried harder. This was all too much for one person.

"She's fine," Garrison said, stroking the kitten's head. "Or at least she will be. See? She already looks better."

Carly did look. The kitten was very light gray with darker gray stripes encircling her thin body. The hair looked healthy enough, if damp. Her unusual blue eyes were alert, too.

"We figured out she needs kitten formula, not cow's milk," Garrison said. "And Mae says I can keep her. I mean, I know we both found her, but I didn't think Mae would let you have a kitten, so..." He trailed off.

Carly figured he was probably right. "Can I hold her?"

"Oh yeah. Of course." Garrison stepped forward and placed the kitten in Carly's cupped hands. She felt it begin to purr and couldn't help but smile. "Her whiskers tickle."

"They do," Garrison agreed, a joyful grin on his face.

They stared at each other. She noticed the way his hair fell into his eyes. He needed a haircut.

He looked down at the floor then. "Uh, I better go. You know, before Mae starts looking for me. It should be dinnertime soon. Do you want her to stay with you? The kitten, I mean. She could keep you company."

Carly snuggled her face in the kitten's fur. She did want her to stay. Then she thought of Paul. What would he do to the kitten? He didn't hurt Carly this time, but he might hurt the kitten. To prove he was serious. Carly pictured the kitten's lifeless body and swallowed hard. She shook her head. "It's okay. You keep her." Carly held the small furry body towards Garrison, fighting tears.

Garrison took the kitten gently, without meeting Carly's eyes. He looked suddenly uncomfortable. "Okay. But, I...uh...I have to lock the door."

Carly glanced at her door, thinking about Paul. He wouldn't be able to sneak up on her again, so for once, she was grateful for the lock. "That's alright," she said, crossing her arms over her chest to hug herself. "I look forward to dinner."

CHAPTER 17

Over the next few days, Garrison fell into a routine when it came to Carly. Each morning, he would bring her breakfast and the kitten. They would stay in her room and let the kitten play. In fact, that first morning, they even named her. He was just explaining to Carly about Mae's unusual reaction to the kitten. "I'm telling you. I don't know who this woman is," he said. "She ordered a litter box, special food, and even toys."

"Why are you so surprised?"

"Because she's..." Garrison paused. He was going to say mean, but that wasn't right. Was strict more accurate? Cold? Sharp? She didn't really seem like any of those things anymore. They were there, but it was as if they were once solid doors now swinging open to reveal someone else.

Carly dragged a chicken feather in front of the kitten. "I think you need to look at a person's actions. Like, for instance, the way she takes care of Tuck, and you. How she is always cooking or cleaning or helping those around her."

It was difficult for Garrison to see Mae that way. "I don't know. She isn't always so nice. I asked if I could use her computer. I mean, she clearly has one with internet. That printout she gave me about kittens had a URL on it. But she said no. She didn't even give me a reason."

Carly shrugged. She lifted the kitten up and turned to him. "So, what should we name her?"

Garrison glanced at the cat and then back at Carly. "I've been calling her kitty."

Carly made an exasperated sound. "That's dull. She deserves a special name."

Garrison tried to think of a special name. He was drawing a blank. He tried for unusual instead. "How about Keegan?" It was the name of a pretty girl in his class.

"That's a boy's name."

Garrison knitted his brow. Sure, Keegan might once have been a boy's name, but now it wasn't. Strange that Carly would be so old-fashioned.

"There are some books over there by my desk," Carly said. "Let's get some inspiration." She stood up, the kitten against her chest. She picked up a green covered novel and flipped through the pages. "Rosaline...Theodora...Hildegard..."

Garrison's mind hung onto the last name — Hildegard. "What about Hilde?"

Carly looked thoughtful. She lifted the kitten to eye level. "Are you Hilde?"

The kitten twitched her whiskers and blinked slowly. Then she started to purr. Carly looked at Garrison, a smile breaking across her face. "I think that's a yes."

Garrison's temperature went up a few degrees in response to her smile. "It's definitely a yes."

After their morning visits, Garrison would run down to the kitchen for the lunch tray. Grabbing it, he would add something from the dining room for himself and they would eat together in Carly's room before venturing out into the yard. They walked from the house to the barn, letting Hilde chase flies or pounce on blades of grass. Garrison loved the way the kitten's antics made Carly laugh. The sound was like a bright light dancing through the air.

And Carly was a great listener. She barely said anything as Garrison told her all about his mother's dream of setting up hospitals in underdeveloped areas. And of his father's high-tech apartment with the latest and best gadgets. How his smartphone controlled his entire house!

But Garrison began wondering about Carly. Whenever he asked her a question, she blamed amnesia and said she remembered nothing about her past. Yet, he stood outside her door once with the breakfast tray, listening to her sing. It was a long song, with several verses, and she seemed to know all the words. He asked her about it later, but she shrugged it off, claiming she didn't recall what she sang.

Another time, he was sitting on her bed as they rolled a jingle bell ball back and forth for Hilde to chase. He asked Carly if she liked the stitching on her bedspread, thinking it was horrible and outdated. She shook her head, explaining it was tatting, sometimes called shuttle lace, but definitely not stitching. And yes, she thought it was beautiful. That surprised him. After all, he didn't know what tatting was. He asked how she knew, but again, she shrugged. Said her memory was foggy and she suddenly couldn't recall.

It felt like a lie.

But why wouldn't she tell him? Garrison didn't know. And he wasn't sure how to ask, not when she looked so happy with Hilde bounding between them. Not when the freckles across her nose winked at him as she smiled, making his heart speed up. He wished Tuck were back. Tuck always seemed to know what to do.

CHAPTER 18

Garrison sat down in the dining room with his plate, staring at the empty seat across from him. It was dinnertime, and he already took Carly her meal. He decided not to stay and visit tonight because he was frustrated, angry that she didn't trust him enough to confide in him. So instead he was here, alternately glaring and pining at Tuck's seat. It was 5 days now that he'd been gone.

Mae, Sam, and Rebecca sat down around him, talking normally. But Garrison continued to stare, wondering where Tuck was right now. And if he was being forced to eat ratatouille, which looked much better in the movie about a rat. Garrison scooped up some red, yellow, and green chunks to examine them. Did Carly like this type of food? Would she even tell him that much truth?

A series of loud pops came from outside. Then a bright light flashed, blinding even through the window. It was in the distance, so Garrison wondered if he'd lost track of the days and it was the fourth of July.

When Mae turned to Sam, Garrison realized that wasn't the case. He saw both of their eyes widen. Then a phone began ringing. The sound was different from the plastic one Mae used to talk to Mrs. Ethelmeyer. Could it be the antique phone making that noise? Garrison didn't realize it still worked.

Mae and Sam shoved back their chairs at the same moment and ran out into the hall. Garrison looked around at Rebecca and the others in the room. Everyone was staring, unsure what to do.

The ringing stopped. But it left an echo in the air, an imprint of tension and malice. The side door slamming made Garrison jump. It also broke the spell. Everyone in the dining room got up to follow.

Outside, the sky was full of a sunset rainbow. It cast dark shadows among the trees and bushes of the forest. Garrison could hear yelling now that he was outside. And screaming. He shivered.

"There," shouted Sam. He pointed to the tree line. If Garrison squinted, there seemed to be a dark shape running towards them. "Get ready, Mae."

She ran across the driveway to the edge of the grass, right where the rougher bushes and trees grew. The property line.

Shouts off to the right drew their attention. "That's the mill to the east," Sam said.

"He's almost here," Mae said to Sam as she stared at the shadow, getting closer. "We need to know what's going on. You go over there and tell them to come around."

"But you don't know all the villagers. How will you know who to let in?"

Mae practically growled. "I'll figure it out!!"

Sam didn't say another word. Instead, he ran around to the back of the house.

Garrison took a few steps towards Mae, squinting into the darkness.

"Stay there!" she commanded. Then she set her feet and bam. A man appeared. "Ralph!" she shouted when she saw him. The relief in her voice was clear. He didn't stop running. When he was about to step out onto the grass, Mae reached out, grasping his upper forearm. She pulled him towards her, as though to hug him, but she didn't. The minute both his feet were in the grass, she stopped.

Ralph started talking immediately. "They're attacking the village. Burning everything."

"The CS?" someone asked from the crowd of onlookers hovering near the house behind Garrison. He didn't know who it was, but he had a faint memory of someone mentioning the CS once before. He couldn't remember where, though.

"Yes! They're a bunch of mercenaries," Ralph yelled to the group.

Swearing and expressions of surprise followed those words. Eyes darted around and a few people hugged themselves.

Garrison turned back to the woods. It was grayer than normal, darker. He sniffed. Smoke. But there was no fire. No village. Was Ralph talking about the town?

"Mae!" a woman yelled. It was like she materialized right there on the spot. Mae turned to her, repeating the same grasping of forearms that she did with Ralph. The woman dropped to the ground, coughing. Garrison recognized her from a day or two before. He didn't know her name, but that hawk nose with the bump in the bridge was unmistakable.

The woman was gasping for breath while forcing out words. "I was eating at the Inn. We smelled the fuel. Then whoosh. Fire was EVERYWHERE!" She coughed again, a horrible wracking sound. "I ran, but there were so many people, I don't know how they could all escape. Outside was chaos. I didn't know what to do. I ran here." Tears started running down the woman's face. "There were so many of them."

"You did the right thing," said Mae strongly. She patted the woman's shoulder. It was an awkward movement. "Rebecca. Can you help her back?"

Garrison watched Rebecca detach herself from the crowd and go towards the woman. She leaned down and helped the woman stand. As they turned towards the house, someone else called Mae. Like the woman, he was just standing there, at the tree line. This man, too, Garrison recognized from earlier in the week. Before Mae could grab his arm, a second man came up and stopped. He fell to his knees right at the edge of the grass, crying out. "Help! Let me in."

It was all so strange. It was like there was an invisible line they couldn't step over unless Mae grasped them.

Another set of loud bangs came from the forest. The sky lit up. Garrison could see the smoke then. Immense columns of gray and more floating in the air. Yet, he couldn't see anything burning. It just wasn't there!

Garrison wasn't sure what to do. He stood and watched as people called out to Mae and she brought them in. Then, they formed small groups on the grass and driveway. Some went to Rebecca on the porch, who was handing out blankets and water.

A man and woman weren't in a group with the others. His attention caught, Garrison moved closer to them, further away from Mae. They were at the very edge of the grass, 20 feet or so to the left of Mae. The woman was wringing her hands and making whimpering noises. Garrison walked closer.

"We shouldn't have left her behind," the woman whispered.

The man, who stood tall and unblinking, answered. "We didn't. We hid her. And she knows where to come. We led them away. Gave her time to escape."

"But what if she didn't escape?"

"She did. Or she will. She'll hide until they're gone. They'll take what they want and leave. And then—"

"Momma!" came a little girl's voice from the darkness in front of them.

The woman lurched forward, but the man grabbed her. "She'll make it. She will."

The little girl was running fast. She wasn't too far off, a light figure in the smoke. The man turned to Mae. "Our daughter. Help!" But Mae was concentrating on another group of people at the property line. She didn't seem to hear.

The woman began clawing at the man's hands, caterwauling. "There's someone chasing her. Oh my God."

The little girl turned to look behind her and stumbled. The woman screamed. "ANGELA! She's not going to make it!"

It was too much for Garrison. He didn't think, he just took off running. Past the woman, past the invisible line they didn't cross. He felt nothing but fear for the girl. She was only a few feet away. Not far at all. He reached her and scooped her up, a small light bundle. He paused briefly to see what was chasing her. At first, it was just a dark shape in the smoke, but then a man materialized. He was dressed in red armor and carried a long pole. He pulled it back to swing and Garrison jerked to the side.

There were more shapes far behind the man in red. Garrison didn't know if they were friends or foes. But more astonishing were the houses, the buildings, the flames. A half mile away, in a small valley, a village was burning. The flames licked upwards out of windows and doors, illuminating everything. Garrison blinked. And there was the forest full of solid trees, but also the village. It made him dizzy, and he lurched sideways. A long pole sailed over his head, just missing him.

The resulting rush of adrenaline helped him focus. The house. He had to get back to the house. It was safe. That's why the people were running there. He would worry about the village later. Right now, he had to get himself and the girl away from the man in red.

He pushed the girl onto his back. "Just hang on." Then he ran faster than he ever had. He could see the house, a solid white beacon. He was so close.

He didn't stop at the edge, didn't veer towards Mae. He simply closed his eyes and ran onto the property, praying it would work.

He expected to feel something as he passed into the grass, a buzz of electricity maybe. An internal alarm bell ringing in his head. But there was nothing.

He stopped and opened his eyes. The woman threw herself on top of him, reaching for the little girl. They all fell over. "Oh Angela," the woman wept. "Oh, my god. Angela."

The little girl reached for her mother and the man helped Garrison up. There were tears shining in the man's eyes. He wasn't as heartless as he seemed. "Thank you," he said, with such a trembling voice, Garrison turned away, uncomfortable. That's when he saw the man in red glaring at him.

He was right at the boundary edge, so close to Garrison, it made his heart race. The man reached out a hand, fingers extended to pass through the air between them. But it met resistance. The man looked to be straining, trying to force his fingers in. Then he quickly pulled his hand away, shaking it as though it burned. His eyes narrowed at Garrison, the hatred in them clear. He turned and ran back to the village and the mayhem.

Garrison realized he was holding his breath and took a deep lungful of air.

"How did you do that?" asked Paul from behind him.

Garrison turned. Everyone was staring at him, including Mae. "She was pretty light," he said.

"No. I mean—"

More shouts came. Urgent calls.

"Sam?" It was a plea.

Sam stepped towards Garrison, nodding. "This way," he said.

Sam led Garrison to an area on the other side of the house. "Just stand here. Don't take a step forward into that tall grass. Do you hear me? Not one step. Okay, here comes someone. Yes, I know him. You can bring him over."

Garrison wasn't really listening, because as he looked out, instead of trees and shrubs, he saw the ghost image of a wooden fence and pasture beyond. There was an immense building with a windmill on top. Smaller buildings, or maybe houses, were on criss-crossing roads leading up to it. The scene was like something out of a really detailed PC game. But in addition to the mill and buildings, he also saw forest trees. Not around the buildings, but overlaid on top of them. He felt the way one did staring at something really close to your eyes, such as your hand. If you focus on it, you see one hand. But if you look out at the distance, you see two.

"Garrison!" Sam's sharp voice snapped him out of it.

A man was running towards them, arms flailing.

Garrison stood ready.

The man extended his arm, and then thud. The man was on the ground.

"You need to reach out to them as they come," Sam chided. "He can't cross without your aid."

Garrison reached down through the boundary, again feeling no sensation, and grabbed the man's arm. The man yanked, likely attempting to stand up, and nearly pulled Garrison over. Sam grabbed his shirt just in time.

Garrison gave one final tug, and the man lurched forward. It was a little like pulling something through a pool, then it was over. The man dropped to the ground, breathing hard.

"Good," Sam said. "Now. Here comes someone else. Hmmm. He's not one of the queen's vassals, but is certainly fleeing. I guess, let him in."

"Why don't I go out there and meet him? Bring him across like I did with the little girl."

"No!" Sam's voice was sharper than Garrison ever heard it. "It puts you at too much risk," he said a bit more calmly. "We're only safe on this side of the boundary. Don't step an inch on the other side. You've endangered yourself enough for one night."

They spent the next 10 minutes there, at the edge of the farmhouse property, Mae and Garrison pulling people in by the arms. More and more people. Garrison wondered if it was the entire village. He was trying to ignore the buildings and trees, and instead focus on the people coming towards him. It made him less dizzy.

Other than the man in red armor, the CS didn't give chase or even approach the farmhouse. "Why don't they follow them? Or come here and try to block the people escaping?" Garrison finally asked Sam.

"I'm not sure," Sam said, the words slow, like he was deep in thought. "Maybe they aren't trying to capture anyone. Some mercenaries just raid, and destroy."

"But the girl?"

"Possibly a crime of opportunity. This isn't a trained army, it's a group of swords for hire. Criminals." The last word dripped with snake venom.

Garrison shivered again.

Eventually, the sun completely set. And the world quieted. And no one else came.

Sam put an arm over Garrison's shoulder. "You did well, lad." Then he went to join Mae.

Garrison didn't remember the last time a man hugged him, even a half hug. His father certainly didn't. Not since he was a small child. It felt odd. He was mulling it over when he heard what Mae said to Sam. "At least the boundary seems strong. We're safe here." She turned and started ordering people into the house.

CHAPTER 19

Garrison paced in his room. He could understand why Sam and Rebecca were in Mae's room, discussing what happened. But why wasn't he invited? He helped, didn't he? He had whatever made Mae special. Now, he could see things that wasn't there yesterday. He glared at his window. The light was on inside, so he only saw his reflection, but still. It was out there.

As he made another loop, an image of the flames sprung into his mind and the echoes of screams. In truth, he felt shaky, like he couldn't settle down. Even petting Hilde didn't work. The danger still seemed to be around him, and he felt like he was being watched.

He suddenly wondered if Carly was alright. Of course, the logical side of his brain said. She was locked in her room the entire time. She was fine.

He turned around and kept pacing. Maybe he should go to Mae's room and demand an explanation. Of course, then

Mae might decide to lock him in, instead of just telling him to stay put. This was preferred to being a prisoner.

A small cry stopped him in his tracks. He turned around and saw Hilde watching him. She opened her mouth and cried again. He ran over. "What's the matter, girl?"

She began scratching at the baseboard. Garrison looked at it closely and noticed part of it was coming away from the wall. Just the bottom, about 12 inches or so from the corner. He could just see the fluff of her favorite stuffed mouse in the hole. She pawed at the wood, but it held firm.

"Did you lose your toy?" Garrison cooed at her.

Hilde meowed back.

He scratched her behind her ears. "Alright. I'll get it for you." With two fingers, he reached into the gap, but the small toy was too far in. He curled his fingers under the loose part of the baseboard and pulled, hoping to make the gap wide enough for him to reach inside. For a moment, nothing happened. Then, the paint holding the baseboard in place gave way. The entire section came flying off, causing Garrison to fall backwards.

Hilde rushed in. She grabbed her toy mouse and made a small chirp. One ferocious claw threw it into the air and it flew in another direction. Hilde scampered after it. Garrison absently noticed all this, because he was staring at what he just revealed. A hidden compartment with a box resting inside.

The space was only 2 inches high and went from one wall stud to the next, with the box filling it. A layer of thick dust told him the box was there for a while. He wondered just how long. Had the house builders left it? Was there a treasure inside? He reached in, ignoring the sticky cobwebs, and pulled it out.

The box was wood with interlocking corners and maybe 8 inches deep. A small brass latch on the front kept it closed. Again, the feeling of being watched washed over him. He looked around. Hilde was staring at him. She blinked her blue eyes slowly and purred. "Does that mean you think I should open it?" he asked.

She purred louder.

Holding the box in his hands, he put his thumbs by the latch. He took a deep breath, as though it were an ancient booby-trapped relic. Then he flicked the latch open.

Nothing happened.

There was no strange wind, no ominous music, and no sand mummy to put a curse on him. To be honest, he was a bit disappointed. He lifted the lid.

Inside were papers. He sifted through them and picked up a photograph near the top. It was of two little girls. They smiled, arms over one another's shoulders. Clearly, it was taken at the farmhouse because Garrison could see the red barn in the background. The girl on the left looked familiar. In fact, it looked like his mom. Something clicked in his brain and the girly room suddenly made sense. What if this was his mom's old room? The pink was probably bright 20 years ago, or whenever she last lived here.

He returned to the box, finding a couple old birthday cards with her name, some notes scribbled on spiral notebook paper, an aced anatomy test, a hand-drawn map of the yard, several certificates awarding Rachel Redapple citizen of the quarter from Biley Prep & Boarding School, and, finally, another photograph. This one was older, faded. It was of a man standing in front of a classic car. Garrison was almost certain it was the one in the barn under a tarp. He flipped the photo over and saw the word Dad written in large, scribbly letters.

He put everything back in the box, smiling. Would his mom remember it and her secret hiding spot? He should take it with him when he went home. She would probably love to see her old keepsakes.

A phone began ringing. Garrison's heart reacted like it was a gunshot, because he recognized the ring. It was the same one as before the attack. He stood, raced to the door and shut it tight before bolting towards the kitchen.

CHAPTER 20

Carly fluttered her wings. She was about to come down from her hiding place at the top of Garrison's large window.

When the shouting began an hour ago, she felt trapped in the little blue prison that was her room. She convinced herself that the commotion was Devose coming for her and she was desperate. She turned herself into a bird. Since her clothes didn't transform with her, she left them, planning to find more later. Right now, she just needed to fly from the house to escape. Luckily, in such an old house, there were larger than normal gaps and she could squeeze under her bedroom door in this shape. She flew silently through the halls as people streamed outside. She sailed right over their heads and through the open side door.

Outside, she paused on the peak of the roof to get her bearings. That's when she realized what was happening. The battle was outside the boundary, not within. She watched, certain now she did not want to leave. She was still perched there when Garrison ran through the boundary to save the little girl. It was so brave of him. He was such a caring person.

When everyone returned to the house, she followed. She knew it would be best to return to her room before someone thought to check on her, but she didn't. Instead, she followed Mae, who was leading Garrison back to his room. Mae told him to stay inside until she came back to explain. Carly remained as well. She watched Garrison pick up Hilde and pace. Put Hilde down and pace. When he discovered the hidden compartment, she almost flew down next to him for a closer look, but thought he would have too many questions.

Now that he was gone and everyone was distracted by the ringing phone, it was the perfect time to escape back to her room. She extended her wings and leaned out. Then the door opened.

She almost fell off the window frame, but her tiny claws held fast. Paul crept into Garrison's bedroom. Carly held her breath.

After a moment, Paul headed to the box full of photos and papers as though it called to him. He rifled through them. Was he searching for something? How did he even know about the box? It must have been his gift. He talked about being able to feel it in his skin.

Paul pulled out a drawing and stared at it. He shivered. Then his face broke out into a sneer. It was not a pleasant sight.

Shoving the paper down into his shirt, Paul closed the box and snuck back out the door. Before he closed it, Carly glided through, flying along the top of the empty hallway. She heard voices in the kitchen, and that's where Paul appeared to be headed, so she landed on the chandelier by the main stairs. She should go up, sneak back into her room. But Paul's actions felt ominous. What did he want with a child's drawing? It was a mystery, but she knew one thing. It wasn't for anything good. Garrison was in for trouble and that bothered her. She decided she would make one of the good luck charms her grandmother taught her about. From the look of things outside the Wagon Wheel Farm, they were going to need all the luck they could get.

CHAPTER 21

When Garrison got to the kitchen, Mae was just hanging up the odd bell-shaped receiver of the antique phone. "What's happening?" he asked.

She turned, and he was surprised to see her smiling. "It's Tuck. He's in the village. He's going to make a run for the farm." She grabbed her coat and a flashlight from next to the side door and headed out. Garrison decided to follow her.

"Isn't he worried about the mercenaries?" Garrison asked as they descended the stairs.

Mae snorted. "Tuck doesn't worry about much. And he's good at sneaking."

Garrison agreed. He kept his eyes on the grass. Otherwise, the double image made his insides knotted. "Do you see double too? It's making me sick."

Mae glanced at him. He could see her eyes, shining in the glow from the flashlight, but her features were invisible.

"Not anymore. With practice, you can control it. Focus on one or the other. Before that, I ate a lot of candied ginger."

Garrison shook his head. "Candied ginger?"

"It settles nausea." Mae waved the comment away. "Never mind. It just takes practice."

"Great."

"I tried to protect you."

He eyed her.

She sighed. "I'm being defensive. It's just that now you've started down the path; it opens you up to danger. Especially because you can't control it. I didn't have to worry about it with your mother. She couldn't see them, but you..." she trailed off.

Garrison didn't know what to say. He felt guilty, but wasn't sure that was right. He couldn't help being able to see them, yet somehow, he felt like he should have done something differently. Should have stopped it. "But what triggered it?" he asked. "I mean, all the sudden, I see both."

"When you crossed the boundary into their world."

Garrison rolled that around in his mind. She had made that boundary pretty clear from the start. Had she been trying to protect him with it?

"But when I went to town, I crossed it."

"You used the driveway. Actually, even if you didn't, most of the front leads only to the human world. This property is a sort of bridge."

"So it's because I went across in the back."

"After that little girl, yes."

That one action changed everything. And they were heading back there again, to the property line at the edge of the lawn.

Mae stationed herself where she had earlier, but this time, Garrison stood beside her. Someone was coming towards them. It was full dark now, but the person was carrying a lantern. The silhouette was shorter than a man and the hair was short and spiky. Garrison couldn't help but smile.

Tuck got to the edge of the property and barely said hello before Mae reached across and grabbed him. She pulled him hard, and he fell into her across the boundary. It almost looked like she was trying to hug him. But within an instant, she was standing him straight up and glaring. "What were you thinking? It's the middle of the night. The village is overrun with mercenaries."

Garrison felt his mouth drop open. So Mae was worried about Tuck, despite her reassurances.

"I know, I know," Tuck said in a placating tone. "I was supposed to go to the town and warn them, you too. The queen's army with me. But when we got close, we realized we were too late. They're still there, dispelling the raiders. But, I was worried about what happened here, so I called from the Inn."

Mae sniffed and rubbed at her face. "We're fine. Safe. We've got refugees from the village as well as those who are usually here, which means we're a bit full."

"My room?" Tuck practically groaned.

"It's my room," Mae said. But it was light with humor. "And it's just got Garrison in it." She motioned towards him and Tuck turned. Garrison pounded him on the shoulder with his fist, swallowing the emotions threatening to make his eyes tear up.

Tuck rubbed at his arm. "Missed me then?"

There was an awkward silence.

"That's enough," Mae said. "Come on. Let's get to bed."

Garrison led the way to the room. When he opened the door, he realized he left his mother's box on the floor. He rushed over and pushed it back into the wall with his foot.

Tuck didn't seem to notice. He went straight to his bed and put down his bag.

Garrison pushed the baseboard back into position while his back was turned.

"What is that smell?" Tuck asked, sniffing the air. He looked around. "There! It's coming from there." He pointed to the litter box. There was a small smelly clump right in the middle. "What is that?"

Garrison snickered a little as he went over to get the scooper. "Uh. A litter box."

"Yeah," Tuck replied, crossing his arms. "But what's it doing in our room?"

"It's for Hilde."

"Who, I presume, is a cat?"

Garrison scooped the offending material into a bag and tied it shut. "Yeah. She's a kitten, actually. Carly and I found her stuck in the compost bin. I kind of adopted her."

"You've been spending time with Carly? As in the girl who mysteriously showed up here and claims not to remember anything?"

Tuck's tone of voice was different, cold. Garrison turned to face him. "I know a lot about her. I've spent nearly every day with her since you left."

Tuck was frowning. "Garrison, this isn't like...like meeting a girl in your world."

"What's that supposed to mean?"

"You can't trust her. You only just met her."

"I only just met you this summer."

"I'm different."

"Why?"

Tuck stepped forward. "You honestly have to ask me that?"

Garrison didn't know what to say. He felt like his skin was on fire along the back of his neck. He didn't know why he was so angry, but he didn't want Tuck talking about Carly. "Whatever." Scooping up Hilde, he left.

First, Garrison walked towards the study, but someone was closing the doors. He could make out some sleeping bags on the floor and there were several voices murmuring inside. He turned around and headed towards the dining room.

The tables were pushed off to the sides and blankets were mounded in the center, people rolling them out into makeshift beds.

He kept going down the hall until he reached the kitchen. He put Hilde down by her food dish. "Want some fresh water, girl?"

Hilde yawned with a full set of needle-like white teeth.

He picked up the bowl and refilled it. What was he going to do if Tuck didn't want to keep her? She could stay with Carly, he supposed. He glanced over and saw her asleep in her food dish. It was the most adorable thing he ever saw. He knew he couldn't give her up. She wasn't just a kitten. She was more. But Tuck was important to him, too.

He sat on the floor by Hilde. For a long time, he stayed there, stroking her sleeping body as the house grew quieter and quieter. Eventually, he was so tired, his thoughts slowed. Only then did he pick Hilde up and sneak back into his room. Tuck was in his bed, his breathing steady. Garrison tried not to make any noise as he got ready to sleep. As he tucked himself and Hilde in, he glanced once more over to Tuck. He hoped Tuck would be in a better mood in the morning so they could work things out.

CHAPTER 22

Carly hopped from one bird foot to another, thinking. She needed some acorns, but there weren't any on the property. She would have to go across the boundary to find an oak tree. Did she dare? Could she return? She was fairly sure, thanks to the memory of Sune telling her to fly, that she could get through the boundary. But was it because she was close to unconsciousness? Or a bird?

She hopped closer to the invisible property line. She didn't want to get stuck out there, with Devose's men so close. They might find her and take her back to him. Then what? She shuddered and sunk down into her warm body feathers.

It would be okay, she told herself. She got through once, she could get through again. It was worth the risk. She took a deep breath, which made a whistling sound through her beak, and launched herself into the air.

She felt nothing as she went through. Not even a tingle. She smiled to herself. This would be easy. She soared into the night sky. Flying felt effortless.

It was easy to locate an oak tree. They were big and broad, growing on the edges of fields. She dived, scooping a few acorns up in her claws. Then she angled back to the farm.

There it was, the boundary. High in the air with her avian vision, she swore she could almost see it now, a shield around the house and yard. The color was unlike any she knew, somewhere in a purple black that made little sense to the normal part of her brain. Then she was at it, sailing through, and pain coursed through her body.

She fell, her limbs no longer feathers, but arms. Her legs felt long and awkward instead of short and powerful. It was lucky she was only a short distance from the ground, because she smacked into it hard. She rolled onto her back, trying to catch her breath.

The grass scratched at her bare skin, but she couldn't do much about it. The only thing she could do was blink and breathe. She focused on the stars in the sky to fight the nausea brought on by the pain. As it receded, she noticed the cold air rushing over her bare skin. She shivered and sat up, glancing around. She was suddenly conscious of being naked, but here was no one around. Would she have bruises this time? She doubted it. The boundary transforming her back into her body was a surprise, and it explained why she was naked the day they found her. But not the bruises. The pain was different. Crossing the boundary felt like all her cells were on fire. It was like the boundary knew she wasn't a bird, way down deep inside, and once it reached that part of her, she exploded.

The acorns! She scrambled around on the grass, hoping they made it through the boundary. She didn't want to have to cross it again. They were there, just next to her on the grass. She clutched them to her chest and sighed.

Glancing at the house, she saw lights on in a few of the windows. That meant she couldn't return to her room in this form, especially naked. She closed her eyes and imagined herself a bird again. Her body shrinking, her nose becoming a beak, her arms growing feathers, her legs scales and claws. She wasn't sure the images were necessary, but it was how her mother taught her to shape change. She could do it too, Carly remembered, another shape-shifter. That's why they moved around so much. They were unusual, and most people didn't trust them. Carly recalled living in old broken huts and gathering wild edibles. How long had they done that? Then they met Devose and everything changed. He took them in. Gave them an entire wing in his mansion. She had the best of everything, right up until the day her mother died.

Carly glanced towards the distant village. There were some smoldering buildings in the darkness, but it was quiet now. Well past midnight, she guessed. Her heart, beating more quickly as a bird, felt hollow. She was engaged to the man who did all this. To the man who killed her mother. It was her blood that he wanted in order to turn back from a deer. Shape-shifter blood, freely given. Her mother had given it all. Yet Devose still had the head of a stag. Now he wanted her blood, too.

Something still bothered her, though. Why the sudden demand to marry on the day her mother died? He could have waited. She would grow up eventually. She couldn't understand why he was so impatient.

Carly turned away from the village. She pushed resolve up over her troubled heart to help her focus on what she had to do next. She had to find some metal, hopefully brass or copper. The house would have some, but there were so many people there. She knew she would be spotted.

She made a small circle, looking out into the darkness. The barn was close by. As she stared at it, considering its likely contents, a soft hooting came from the roof. An owl, she thought. Then her heart raged wildly in her chest. Owls ate small birds, as well as mice.

Immediately, she elongated her body, growing a tail and pointy snout. Her feathers became fur and her limbs became four legs with small hand-like paws. She looked at the barn again with her raccoon eyes. The owl was far off to one corner. She grabbed the acorns in one paw and used the other three to move towards the barn. She traveled close to the bushes and shadows to stay hidden. Near the barn door, the owl turned to look at her. Its eyes were bright in the darkness.

She stood on her hind legs, making herself as tall as possible.

The owl blinked at her.

She bared her teeth.

The owl turned away, rotating its head unnaturally far to the other side, and she skittered to safety.

In the barn, she stayed a raccoon. It was easier to open doors and move objects with her slim fingers. Plus, they had great night vision.

She found what she was looking for in a tidy workshop behind an old car. Some gold wire, thin enough for her to twist and turn, even with tiny paws. It would be perfect to wind into a fumsup charm. She was giddy with excitement. The last time she made one was when she was a very little girl with her grandmother. "Mountain ash is best for luck," she told Carly in a voice like a waterfall. "But I prefer oak. It's easier to find the seeds and doesn't just ward off misfortune. It offers the wearer strength of character in difficult times too." Her grandmother removed the small acorn cap from the seed and held it in her hand. "We carve a small horseshoe on the back, always open upward to catch the luck." She used the edge of a small knife to make the half circle shape. Then, she plucked a single hair from her head. "You need to put a bit of yourself in it too, to make it work." She spit on the hair and rolled it into a ball. Then she placed it on the acorn seed and returned the cap. "The body was originally cast metal," she went on, "but I use thin drawn-out metal instead. It's more flexible and lets me create any shape I want. See?" She held up a wire stick figure. "It used to be that fat, chubby babies were luckiest, but styles change. Now the long limbs of fantasy creatures are more popular."

"Will you sell this one, Grandmama?" Carly remembered asking.

Her grandmother smiled at her. "No, dear. This one is for you. Promise me you'll wear it every day."

Carly couldn't believe her luck. Grandmama's charms were valuable. To get one for free was a dream come true.

"Now, pay attention so you can make your own someday. Shape the body in any way that pleases your customers. The gender, nor the shape, is truly important. It's the thumbs." She wrapped the edges of the wire around some nails in a board to create a mitten shape at the end of the figure's arms. Using a stick, she curled the thumb upwards. "There. Now, sweetheart, go get some of your mother's lace. We'll dress your charm up nice."

A hiss brought Carly back from her memory. Another raccoon was in the barn and not happy. She wished that, along with her shapeshifting, she could understand different animal languages, but she couldn't. The hiss was pretty clear, however. GET AWAY. Carly crossed to the other side of the barn on two legs. This seemed to bother the other raccoon, who hissed again and ran off.

Idly, she wondered where her grandmother's charm was, but then recalled what happened. Her mother and she sold it for food money a year later, after her grandmother died. Carly's chest felt tight from the loss, like it happened in this moment, instead of years ago. She focused on her plan instead. She would have to sneak back into the house. But how? All the doors and windows were closed. Maybe if she turned into something small, a mouse, she could find a gap. That seemed like the best option.

The owl was gone when she emerged from the barn, so she shrank. Tinier paws, a flexible body, and a thin tail. She shoved the acorns in her cheeks and picked up the wire with her mouth as she ran on all four feet across the yard. Her night-accustomed eyes went immediately to a small gap in the siding, where the slats met the rocks and mortar of the basement. If she could get in there, she could make her way back upstairs.

It was a tight fit, even as a mouse. She pushed the acorns and wire in first, shoving her body through afterwards. Still, she made it. And the house was quiet now. She climbed down the wall, using the rough stones as footholds, wire and wood back in her mouth. Then she scrambled up the basement stairs, squeezing easily under the door. She traveled along the baseboards and walls to avoid anyone stepping on her, although no one was out. She glanced towards Garrison's room. It was dark and quiet. The whole house was quiet, the eerie kind that comes in the late hours of night or very early hours of morning. Even the clock in the hallway seemed to whisper the minutes. She scampered up the stairs towards her room. It would take her the rest of the night, but she would make them each a fumsup.

CHAPTER 23

In the morning, Garrison woke up to an empty bedroom — Tuck was gone. He lay back down, defeated. That's when someone knocked on the door.

"Garrison!" Mae yelled through her rapping. "It's past breakfast. Don't you want to take Carly's tray up?"

Garrison sat straight up. "Yes. Coming," he yelled. He pulled on some shorts and a t-shirt. Finger-combing his hair, he opened the door.

Mae was standing there with furrowed brows. "I thought you were being responsible?"

"It was a late night!" He took the tray from her.

She crossed her arms. "For all of us. Yet, here I am."

Garrison really didn't think that was fair, but he decided not to say anything. Instead, he stole a piece of toast from Carly's tray. He noticed there was more than usual, about double, actually. "It was just one time," he said with a full mouth. "Won't happen again."

Mae gave him an *it-better-not* look and turned away.

"Wait, Mae." He paused, not knowing if he should ask the question. What if she didn't answer? But Tuck was gone, so Mae was his only option for answers. "I want to know something. About last night. When Tuck came back, he mentioned an army trying to stop an attack. But why did they attack us?"

Mae sighed. "Technically, they didn't attack us. They raided a village in their world, not ours. The queen's spies discovered the plan, and she dispatched the army, along with Tuck, but they were a day late."

"And the people that ran here, ran from the attackers, the CS, they came here because..."

"Because it's surrounded by an ancient protection. No one can get in if I—" she paused, "if one of us doesn't let them in."

Garrison thought about how the man bounced off the invisible boundary last night. How the little girl's parents just stood there at the edge, unwilling to cross. About the way the man in red armor reacted, like his hand burned. "Except someone did make it in." Carly. She showed up on the grass, inside the boundary. Days ago.

Mae pushed her lips together. "Yes. Someone did."

"That's the real reason you keep Carly locked in that room, isn't it?"

"Yes. And no. We don't know how she did it. Or what she is doing here. But I also know someone beat her. She's safer locked away from them, at least until her memory returns. Then maybe we can get some answers." Mae furrowed her brow. "Her memory hasn't come back, correct? You would tell me if she remembered things?"

Garrison swallowed hard, but forced himself to maintain eye contact. "She remembers little things here and there. Nothing big. Not like that."

Mae nodded and looked away.

Garrison felt relieved. He didn't want Carly to get in trouble. But he knew she remembered more than she told him.

"The rulers of their realm think that if they send enough good into ours, it will be reflected in their own. That it will defeat the army of the enemy."

"Really?"

Mae shrugged. "Love, unity, forgiveness. Those are powerful. The people that use this house to enter our world spread those. They go to places of conflict and push for mediation, for peace. Not just in this country, but all over the world."

Garrison blinked. "So all the people that stay here are trying to bring about world peace?"

Mae nodded. "It's an easy crossing point. They enter from their world, stay one night, and leave the next day in ours. I do my best to make it a comfortable transition."

Garrison shook his head. He thought about his mother. She left this summer because she wanted to help people in developing countries. Her plan was to travel far away and use her medical training to make a difference. Now, here was his grandmother, who hadn't left her house in years and she was orchestrating world peace. It was mind-boggling.

"Do you think the plan will work?" he finally asked her. "That peace here will stop the war there?"

"I don't know because I've never been to their world. I just know ours and am happy about any way to make it better. Now. Get a move on. Carly's waiting."

Garrison nodded. "Let me just grab Hilde."

He turned around, but he didn't see her. She wasn't under the covers or using the litter box. He put Carly's tray down and looked under the beds, the dressers — everywhere. He even glanced at the loose baseboard, but it was tucked in place. Then he had an awful thought that Tuck could have done something to her. Almost instantly, he chastised himself. Tuck wouldn't do that.

Mae cleared her throat. "Cats are expert at hiding. I'm sure she's in here. Just shut the door. You can find her later."

Garrison gave the room one last look, but knew she was right. Probably. He grabbed the tray and headed upstairs.

CHAPTER 24

Carly glanced out the window. It must be late morning. Where was Garrison? She paced the small room until, finally, there was a knock on the door. "Come in!"

Garrison unlocked the door and opened it. "Sorry, Carly. I know I'm late, I—"

She didn't let him finish. She was too excited. "I have something for you," she said, taking the tray and putting it on the dresser. Then she pulled the fumsup from her dress pocket and showed it to him. "See, its head is an acorn turned on its side. The little pointy nub becomes its nose, and I penned in some eyes. I used gold wire for the body and wrapped it in colored string to make the pants and shirt."

Garrison stared at it with no obvious expression.

Carly frowned. She pushed it into his hand. "It's a good luck charm. Soldiers used to wear them into battle on their coat buttons. That's why there's a metal loop on the back."

Garrison turned it over to see the loop. "Um, my coat has a zipper," he muttered.

Carly stepped back. She was sure he would like it. She pushed down the tears that sprung to her eyes. "Forget it. I can take it back."

"No, no," Garrison said. "I like it." He stuck it in his pocket. "It's just that I'm distracted. There was an attack last night. Not on us, I guess, but on the village nearby." He glanced at her, a question in his eyes.

She didn't know why. Was he asking her if she knew about the village? Or the attack? She decided to be vague. "I heard some commotion last night." She took a piece of toast off the tray. "Is everyone okay?"

"I don't know." Garrison walked over to her window and looked out. "Can I ask you something?"

"Sure," she said.

Garrison took a moment to speak. He moved his right hand over his chest and rubbed his left shoulder. It seemed like a nervous gesture. Finally, he said, "That village out there. The one you know about. Well, for me, it just appeared. Suddenly. When I crossed the boundary to rescue a little girl. Now I can't look outside without feeling sick to my stomach. Why? I mean, what does it mean?"

Her heart went out to him. She couldn't imagine suddenly being able to see invisible things, dangerous things, and unable to do anything about it. "Sometimes not knowing is better," she whispered.

Garrison glanced up quickly. His eyes changed from soft and sad to hard and angry. "Is it?"

The atmosphere in the room grew thorns. Carly stood up straighter.

Garrison kept eye contact. "You knew I was different. From the first moment we met. You said something about the silver eyes. Orbs. The sight."

Carly bit her lip and glanced at the door. Was Paul out there, listening?

"Carly?"

She swallowed. "There are some humans that can see us. They have silver eyes. That's all. Everyone knows it."

Garrison clenched his jaw. "And how did you get across the boundary?"

She took another step back, surprised. This wasn't what she was expecting. "I've told you. I don't remember." She winced, having said the words automatically, but they were a lie. She did know.

"Don't remember? Or am I better off not knowing?"

Carly felt trapped. She couldn't tell him. Paul would know and tell everyone about her being engaged to Devose. Shapeshifters were feared and loathed. No one would take her side. She would be banished.

He took a step towards her and she backed away further. "Before, I didn't really understand why it was a big deal," he said. "I mean, people were coming through all the time. My mom. Me. The Ethelmeyer lady." He shook his head. "But last night, I saw a man running full speed hit that invisible barrier and bounce off. Yet you, somehow, magically, got across."

"I can't."

"Can't? Or won't?"

She heard the crack in his voice. This was about more than the boundary. Still, she said nothing.

He pushed past her, slamming the door. The key in the lock never sounded so final. Carly threw herself on the bed and cried.

CHAPTER 25

Garrison knew she was lying. What he didn't know was why? Did Carly think she was protecting him from something? Or was she using him? Was their friendship fake? He practically choked on the pieces of his shattered heart. He really liked her, and knowing she was lying to him was almost too much.

He went outside and saw Tuck sitting in a chair on the porch. "Did you do something to my cat?" he demanded.

Tuck raised his eyebrows. Garrison knew it was because of his aggressive tone. He never spoke that way to anyone. But today was a new day, a new Garrison. One that didn't get taken advantage of by these stupid invisible beings. "Did you?"

"No," said Tuck. "She was at the door and I let her out."

Garrison groaned. "You can't let her out."

"Why not? She's a cat."

"She's a baby cat. She might get lost or stuck or make a mess somewhere." Garrison huffed and went back inside the house. "Hilde," he called. "Hilde."

Tuck was following. "Well, excuse me. I didn't brush up on interloping kitten etiquette. And, by the way, what's your problem?"

"You lost my cat."

"I don't think that's it."

Garrison ignored him. "Hilde?" he called as they entered the kitchen.

"She's here," said Mae, pointing to Hilde poised on a stool by the window. She was motionless except for the very tip of her tail. A bird was standing on the porch railing, staring back at her.

"Why didn't you tell me she was here?" Garrison demanded, picking Hilde up and cuddling her to his chest.

Mae's face turned sour. "I was planning on it when you brought the breakfast tray back from Carly's room. Where is it?"

Garrison turned and started walking away, trying to soothe Hilde, who was squirming. "I left it there," he said over his shoulder.

"Hold on. You've never left it there before. Usually, you spend hours with her. What happened?"

Garrison didn't stop. "Nothing," he growled, marching back to his room.

Tuck came in several minutes later, but Garrison ignored him. He dragged a feather across the bed for Hilde.

Tuck went to the other bed and started strumming on his guitar. "Do you want to talk about it?" he asked.

"No."

"Good."

That made Garrison laugh a little. "Hey, will you come with me to take Carly lunch in an hour?"

"Happy to," Tuck said.

Garrison tried to read something in his tone, but couldn't. Tuck would be an excellent poker player. Still, knowing Tuck would be there made Garrison relax. He wouldn't have to face Carly on his own because he didn't think he could do it. He didn't want to like her, not anymore. It would be easier to be distant with Tuck there.

CHAPTER 26

Carly's stomach rumbled. She thought Garrison must be late. Again. Was he even going to come? He left so angry, maybe he wouldn't.

There, a knock. Not his normal one. This one lacked the happy energy he usually had. Or was she reading too much into a knock?

"Come in."

The lock clicked, and the door opened. Garrison walked in first, but without a lunch tray. Then another boy entered — Tuck. He held the tray. Carly's heart fell from her chest and plopped into her stomach, and acid splashed up into her mouth. She pushed it down and forced herself to smile. She turned to Garrison.

He was looking at the floor, a deep crease between his eyebrows. She let go of her smile. "What's wrong?"

His gaze turned to her face, but he wasn't seeing her. She stepped into his personal space and reached her arms out to shake him.

"That's close enough," Tuck said.

She glared at him. What did he know? She and Garrison were friends.

Garrison stepped back from her. "Nothing," he said.

She narrowed her eyes at him. "You're lying."

"You would know."

Carly reeled. How could he say that? Her chest burned, sending tears up to her eyes.

Tuck put the tray on the dresser. "How did you get across the boundary?"

She wanted to punch him. He was the reason Garrison was acting so coldly, Carly was certain. "I don't know." It didn't even feel like a lie, saying it to him. It felt like an act of defiance.

"I think Mae should bring your meals from now on," Garrison said quietly.

Her eyes darted back to him, to his face. For a moment, she thought she saw the hurt and sadness she was feeling. Then it was gone. He looked away. "Come on, Tuck. Let's go."

Her heart splintered. Shame, sadness, anger all battled to be heard as the door closed behind the two boys and was locked. Maybe she should have told him the truth — about the boundary. About Devose. But the truth would have made him hate her. She touched the tattoo on her shoulder. But it wasn't like she was a spy, an agent of Devose. She wasn't here to hurt anyone. She was running away too. Didn't that matter to Garrison? Didn't he care about her at all? A small voice in her head whispered. Maybe he would, if he knew.

Her attention was caught by a noise as someone tried her doorknob. She watched it turn slowly. Carly sat up straighter, ready to face whoever it was. But the door didn't open. It was locked, and the person obviously didn't have the key. Paul, she thought suddenly. The wind left her lungs. She was afraid of what he would do.

She stood up and walked over to the window. She put the palms of her hands and forehead on the windowpane. The sun was on the other side of the house, casting long shadows on her side. They stretched into the forest, joining the darkness that always hung beneath the heavy canopy. She felt like she had lost everything, but at least she was safe from Devose.

A whisper of paper drew her attention. A note pushed under the door lay on the floor. She went to pick it up and read it. There was one word, written in bold caps.

TONIGHT.

***

There was a knock at the door, and Carly lifted her head. The skin on her cheeks felt tight from dried tears. She didn't say anything, didn't want to see anyone. She knew it wouldn't be Garrison.

The person on the other side didn't wait long. The lock clicked loudly, and the door opened. Mae stood there. She seemed to fill the doorway, although in reality, Mae was only a few inches taller than Carly herself.

Mae scanned the small room.

Carly pushed herself into a sitting position. She barely touched her lunch. It was still on the dresser where Tuck left it. Carly's eyes started to tear. She hated him for turning Garrison against her.

The trays from yesterday's dinner and this morning's breakfast were stacked neatly on the desk, the dishes inside each other to save room.

Mae stepped forward. "Fight?"

Carly felt her heart skip a beat. What was Mae talking about? Tonight? The NOTE? Did she know something? Because Carly certainly didn't. She had no idea what Paul was trying to tell her about tonight.

"What do you mean?" Carly finally asked.

Mae crossed her arms. "I mean, is the reason my grandson isn't here, and isn't bringing my dishes back to the kitchen, because you got into a fight? An argument?"

Carly shook her head."

"You didn't remember something? Tell him something I should know?"

"I didn't tell him anything."

"Not even a little thing that upset him?"

Carly felt the tears well up in her eyes. "No. His friend is back and now he doesn't care about me." She winced at the pathetic wailing sound of her words.

Mae didn't respond again immediately. The silence swelled, filling the space in the room until Carly felt the pressure on her chest. It was suffocating. Mae's eyebrows were pulling at her forehead in a sympathetic expression. Carly thought about all the kindness this woman showed people: her, refugees from the village, even a smelly little kitten. Fresh tears fell from Carly's eyes. She opened her mouth, about to tell Mae everything. How Paul was threatening her. That Devose wanted to marry her and his searches for silver-eyed children, like Garrison.

"Give him some time," Mae said. Then she turned away, heading towards the stacks of dishes.

Carly sagged, a burst balloon. She closed her mouth.

"There's been a lot happening lately. He needs time to absorb it all. Yeah. He just needs time."

As Mae left, Carly lay back down. Time was something she doubted they had.

CHAPTER 27

Garrison stroked Hilde's head. He loved the little kitten, but she also made him think of Carly. Maybe he was being too hard on her. Yes, she was lying to him, but maybe she had a good reason. Maybe she would tell him, given enough time. If she trusted him. That made his stomach cramp up. He thought of all the things he told her, because he trusted her. Inside, was she laughing at him? Did she consider him a fool?

"That cat won't have hair left at the rate you're going," Tuck said from the doorway. "Come on. You need a distraction."

Garrison glanced at his useless portable video game. A distraction would have been nice.

"Be my lookout," Tuck said.

Garrison turned to him again and noticed how he was standing. He was on the balls of his feet, practically vibrating. His eyes were wide and merry.

"Come on, Garrison. You know you want to."

Garrison refused to smile, but he said, "Fine."

They left Hilde in the bedroom, and Tuck led the way to the kitchen. "So, Mae said that someone is sneaking into the kitchen between meals and cutting pieces from her dessert. So we're going to teach them a lesson."

Garrison raised an eyebrow.

"You wait here," he said at the door. "If anyone comes, start a loud conversation with them."

"About what?"

"Whatever. Talk about the hot weather, ask them if they're enjoying their stay, compliment their shoes — anything."

"Their shoes?"

Tuck didn't respond. He went over to the far counter where Mae usually let pies and cakes cool.

Garrison rolled his eyes and pivoted to watch the hallway. At this time of day, he rarely saw people. They were either inside their rooms with fans or outside, in some shady spot in the yard. It wouldn't be busy again until just before dinner. He glanced back at Tuck. "Are you frosting a balloon?" he asked.

"Shut up," Tuck whisper-yelled.

Garrison checked the hallway again. Clear. He turned back. Tuck WAS frosting a balloon. It was somehow wedged into a rectangular cake pan. Garrison wondered if he taped it in there. With a rubber spatula, Tuck was adding globs of white icing. Within minutes, he had the balloon covered and had smoothed the icing. He pulled out a jar of sprinkles from a drawer and shook them over the entire thing. Garrison had to admit, it was pretty convincing.

Tuck came over. "Okay, so we are going to hide in the butler's pantry. We'll see who comes along to satisfy their sweet tooth." He grinned. "It'll be the last time they do, I bet."

Garrison shook his head, a little in awe and a little in disbelief that he was going along with this.

It took about 10 minutes for someone to enter the kitchen who didn't belong there. He headed straight towards the dessert area, too. Garrison couldn't stifle his laugh when the man picked up a knife, so Tuck punched him in the gut. A friendly punch. Mostly.

Garrison slapped a hand over his mouth.

The man carefully positioned the long serrated knife down the middle of the cake. In slow motion, it pushed into the frosting. Garrison counted one second, then the balloon exploded! Sprinkle-flecked frosting flew everywhere. Man, cabinets, counters — all covered. And the man's yell of surprise echoed in the halls. Garrison and Tuck were laughing so hard, it made it difficult to run to their room through the extra door in the dining room. "Did you see that?" Tuck said unnecessarily. "Blam." He used his hands to mimic the popping. "It was awesome."

Garrison nodded. "I loved his face. I think a few sprinkles went up his nose."

They were still belly laughing when Mae stomped into their room. Her hands were on her hips. "You've been back for less than a day, and already mischief."

"Garrison was sulking," Tuck said. "I had to do something."

Garrison looked at him in surprise.

Mae made a noise like a growl. "You are unbelievable. Well, you and sulky Garrison can clean up. It's a mess in my kitchen. Let's go."

They followed, only pretending to feel guilty. In reality, Garrison felt whole again. It was like Tuck never left.

***

At dinner, Tuck told the balloon story to Paul, who hung on every word. Just as he reached the end, a voice echoed loudly through the open windows of the house. A voice Garrison never heard before.

"Mae. Oh, Mae! Come out, come out, wherever you are." It was a man's voice, deep and smooth in the way movie trailer voices are. Yet it made the hair on Garrison's neck stand up. He turned towards Mae. She was looking at Sam. They stood up together.

The voice continued. "Don't make me come in and get you."

"He's in the boundary," someone said. They were at the window, hands held over their eyes to see through the glass, despite lights being on inside.

"Impossible," Mae countered.

"He's heading to the back door."

Mae turned and stomped into the hall. As before, it took a few heartbeats for everyone to follow. Garrison pushed his way to the front and was one of the first to get to the back porch. Mae was at the edge of the very top stair. Her legs were set shoulder-width apart, her knees bent. She looked ready for battle. Opposite her, at the foot of the stairs, was a figure wearing a tight black business suit. It looked to be a man, but his entire silhouette was strange, because of the huge deer head on top of his human-looking shoulders. Garrison thought it was a mask or helmet, but then he saw the eyes blink.

The creature swung its head, looking at the crowd, the enormous antlers whistling through the air. "Cowards," the thing said in the same deep, smooth voice as before. "Your gifts make you gods, but you hide here like scared children, running errands for queen mummy. Well, a new era is approaching. As you can see." He spun around in a circle. "Your little bubble of safety has been popped."

"How?" Mae demanded. Her voice was loud, demanding. "How did you get through?"

The stagman gazed at her and smiled. Garrison grimaced at the strangeness of a deer smiling. "It's really quite an amusingly twisted tale. You might even say a plaiting of fate." He laughed, a cold, emotionless sound that made Garrison shudder.

The stagman took a step forward. He placed a foot on the first step. "Stop," yelled Mae. She removed the bracelet she always wore, unwinding the coils of silver beads. Mae flung it out in front of her like a whip, and everyone behind Garrison stepped back.

"Please. You think that will stop me?" He was calm, in control. Garrison thought he saw Mae's hand shake a little. "You won't win. I've come offering sanctuary, to my kind at least. But you...well, you are unnecessary." He leaned forward, his antlers pointed at Mae's chest. Was he going to charge her?

"Devose, stop," said a loud voice from the back of the crowd. Everyone turned towards it. Garrison thought he knew who it was. He bit his lip and waited.

People parted. And there, at the doorway, stood Carly. She was dressed in strange clothes. In fact, they were his clothes! A pair of loose jeans and his gray Green Bay Packers t-shirt.

Carly glanced towards him. Her eyes widened for a moment, and she screwed up her face. Was she trying to send him a silent message?

She turned away, back to the stagman, whom she called Devose. As Garrison's attention followed, he glimpsed Mae's face before she too turned back. Her eyes were different — glowing. They looked like two silver orbs.

Carly's voice rang out again. "I will go..." her voice trembled, "with you. If you leave now — in peace."

Devose straightened. "Ah, Carly," he said, "Still playing your role? How nice."

"What are you talking about?" she asked.

"Oh, come now. You've been providing information to me for weeks."

"It's not true."

"There's no need to lie about it. You have my mark on your shoulder."

Gasps erupted.

Devose continued. "Everyone here knows the truth. Unless...there is someone special whom you hope still believes in you." He began scanning the crowd.

Tuck suddenly elbowed Garrison in the gut. Air whooshed out of his body and he bent double. Tuck pushed him to the side, behind the legs of some other bystanders.

"There is no one," Carly was saying. "Let's just go."

"In a hurry?"

Carly's voice cracked a bit when she answered. "The deal is only good if you leave right now and don't come back."

"I'm afraid I can't do that. The time of free will is at an end."

"Not mine."

The air was suddenly electric. Garrison struggled to see what was happening. Tuck leaned on him, trying to keep him down. Garrison caught sight of Carly standing at the top of the stairs in front of Mae. She looked so small, so breakable up there. Her arms were crossed. He could see her shivering. Why was she wearing his clothes? And how did she get out of her room?

"I shall return in a week," Devose said slowly.

"Shut your eyes. He's looking again," whispered Tuck. Garrison glanced at him, confused, and Tuck laid all his weight on Garrison, covering his face.

"During those seven days, anyone here is free to join me," said Devose. "The Coalition of the Stag would welcome you. And now. Carly. After you, my dear."

Garrison struggled against Tuck. He wanted to see, wanted to stop Carly. He could hear people whispering behind him. "Well, this proves it, she was a spy...Coalition of the Stag, the CS...Devose is back!"

Garrison managed to get his left eye free. He saw a portion of Devose's legs walking away. And something falling, as though from a pocket. It looked like paper as it floated down to the ground.

No one moved for a full minute. Garrison was counting. Then he heard someone walk down the stairs. Mae came into his line of sight and she picked up whatever it was Devose dropped. She barely glanced at it before yelling, "Garrison? Garrison!"

Tuck moved, releasing Garrison. He stood up slowly as Mae came pounding back up the stairs. As he moved towards her, he tripped, landing against her. She closed her arms around him. "It's okay, Garrison," she said. "We're going to get you away from here."

Garrison wanted to argue with her, to explain that he didn't mean to hug her. But his body wasn't responding right. His nervous system felt jumbled. It was like two different radio stations were playing at once, making a discordant song inside his head. Was this shock?

Mae continued to hold him, pulling him inside. He was dimly aware of Tuck following them into the kitchen.

Garrison felt a stool beneath him, and he sat. Tuck next to him. He heard Mae pull a pan onto the stove. "Hot chocolate. Then I'll call your mother and arrange for a ride back to..."

"He can't go!" cried Tuck.

Mae didn't turn around, but her head dipped. "He has to."

"Why? Isn't he safer here with us? What if Devose finds him?"

"You mean like he unquestioningly will if he stays here?"

"But I just got back." Tuck looked at Garrison, who looked away.

Mae was firm. "My mind's made up."

Tuck pushed back from the kitchen island and stormed off into the hallway, presumably to their room.

The strange jangling inside Garrison's head intensified. He tried to focus on something else.

On the table, in front of him, lay Mae's silver beaded bracelet and the paper Devose dropped. The bit of a picture he could see inside the paper looked familiar. He glanced at Mae, but her back was still to him as she stirred the pot. Garrison swallowed his nerves and reached out. He pulled the paper over and unfolded it fully. It was the map from his mother's memory box. Just a child's drawing. He was disappointed. He was about to refold it when he saw text on the bottom that he hadn't noticed before.

From lioness' beau, dance three pines in a row, then seven paces to go.
Rachel, Explorer Extraordinaire

Garrison got a flash of memory of his mom in the car, telling him about the farm. '*I dug hideouts; hid treasures.*' Was this a map to one of the treasures? How did Devose get it? And why? *Fate,* he'd said. Was it crazy to think the two things were related?

"This map. It was my mom's, right?"

"What?" Mae glanced towards the table quickly. "Yes. Your mom drew it. She used to play pirate in the woods. That was a long time ago. Before this all started."

"Shouldn't we follow it? I mean, the map might lead us to Devose and we can figure out how he got through the boundary."

Mae poured the hot chocolate into two mugs. "Devose dropping that piece of paper wasn't an accident."

"You don't know that," Garrison argued, but even as he said it, he realized the action was no doubt intentional.

Mae handed him a mug. "He wants to pique our interest, wants us to follow that map. It's a trap. Now drink."

Reluctantly, Garrison drank, and the sweet, hot liquid helped with the jangling. His brain cleared. Yet, with clarity, came a strong desire to persevere. There must be something they could do. Some way to stop Devose. He looked at Mae, staring at the table. Clearly, she was lost in thought. He couldn't believe she didn't want to know how Devose could do the impossible. He decided to ask Tuck about it. "I'd like to go back to my room," he said softly. He didn't want to draw her too far from her thoughts. He wanted her to stay distracted and not really notice him.

It worked. Mae nodded, and Garrison drained his mug before heading to his room.

CHAPTER 28

Tuck paced their bedroom. "Wait! Back up. You're telling me that your mom hid an object in the woods that lets Devose across the boundary. And that childhood treasure map you found in the wall leads to it?"

Garrison closed the window drapes. They were just fabric and unlikely to keep anything out, but he did it anyway. It felt better. "It's just an idea."

"But how does Carly fit in? Did she get the map for him? We know she was in our room. She was wearing your clothes!"

Garrison felt his shoulders get tense. Carly. He felt so tangled up inside when he thought about her. Angry. Sad. A longing he didn't want to examine too closely. "I'm not sure she..." he didn't finish.

Tuck considered him. "You heard what Devose said."

"Yeah, but isn't he the bad guy?"

"Definitely. We'll be lucky if he really stays away for the whole week."

"I agree," said someone from the doorway. Garrison and Tuck jumped, but it was only Mae, leaning against the door frame and looking exhausted. "Sorry," she said. "I didn't mean to startle you."

Garrison stepped towards her. "Let's all go back to the city, to my mom's apartment. You can—"

Mae put her hands on his shoulders. "I can't leave," she said. "It's my responsibility to stay here. I need to keep this place safe for as long as I can."

"But he's the man from the legend Tuck told me about. Isn't he? Devose? That God of Darkness guy who wants a world of chaos and war."

Mae turned her gaze away. "He may be, but he can still only nudge. And I've been doing this for a long time. He won't find me as easy to sway as most. I know how to protect myself. But you, Garrison. You're too new to your power. That's why you have to go."

Garrison thought her voice broke a little on the last word. Did that mean something?

"I called your mother, but had to leave a message. When she returns my call, I'll see if your other grandparents are back, or a neighbor—"

"No!"

Mae shook her head. "I don't know what else to do. You don't know how to fight it. There is so much you just don't know."

"Then teach me."

"I don't want that for you. That's why I never wanted you to come here."

It was all Garrison could do not to rub the hole Mae just ripped open in his chest. She didn't want him here, after all they went through. After finding out he was like her. Garrison made his hands into fists. "Yeah. Well. I never wanted to come."

Her eyes looked big and watery, but he didn't care. He ran out of the room, going to the stairs and taking two at a time until he reached Carly's room.

The door was locked.

This made zero sense. He saw her outside. Running down the back stairs, he grabbed the key from a hook in the kitchen. Mae was calling his name, but he ignored her. His heart felt like giant chunks of concrete were falling on it. He wanted answers, especially about Carly. Everything seemed to be going wrong because of her. Garrison had to find her journal.

Inside her room, Garrison noticed her dress on the floor. It was like it had just dropped right there in the middle of the room. He tore through her dresser drawers. There were plenty of other dresses, a few shirts and even a couple pairs of pants. Why did she go into his room for clothes? It wasn't for the map. She already used that. Assuming she took it in the first place.

Searching for the journal, he looked under the bed, felt under the pillows and beneath the mattress. He even searched the tank on the back of the toilet, which was gross.

Nothing.

He sat down on the bed, trying to think of where else to look. A terrible thought struck him. *Maybe she took it with her.* His shoulders slumped. Maybe she really was guilty. He ran his hand along the bedspread. Memories floated to the surface of his mind — laughing with Carly, confiding in her. Her green eyes sparkling with each smile. The day they named Hilde. Garrison looked up to the books she used for inspiration. A few of them were sticking out further than the others. He stood up.

He took out *One Viking's Romance*, a novel in the middle of the bumped out section. He flipped through the text-filled pages. It smelled musty. He turned to put it back and saw a swatch of teal. Clever. Hide a book longways behind other books. He pulled out the small journal. He opened it to the first page when he heard Mae's voice, close and frantic. "Garrison? Garrison!"

He shoved the journal behind his back, tucking it into his waistband. When he cracked the door open, he saw Mae down the hall, near the kitchen stairs. He stepped out of the room, and she immediately saw him. "You're leaving," she said. Actually, she nearly shouted it. And he noticed she had his suitcase.

"Now? It's the middle of the night."

"Yes, now," she said, pushing him towards the main stairs. Which was another odd thing because it meant they would have to pass all the other rooms. Why not just turn around and go back into the kitchen? Garrison opened his mouth to ask, but she pushed him forward.

"Your father's secretary arranged for you to get picked up," Mae said over her shoulder. Garrison looked behind her and saw people leaning out of their rooms. They were putting on coats and hats, suitcases of their own at their feet.

"But it's the middle of the night," he repeated, as she rushed him down the stairs. "This makes no sense. She doesn't—" He trailed off as he saw Hilde loose at the bottom. He scooped her up. He wasn't leaving without her. Maybe he could guilt his father into letting Hilde stay there. He turned towards the front door.

"No. This way," Mae whispered. She pushed him towards the back of the house. Garrison didn't understand at all, but she kept shushing him when he tried to ask.

Before they reached the back door, Mae opened one off to the right. It led to a large bedroom. There was some antique furniture, a no-frills full size bed and two glass doors leading to the outside. Garrison knew instantly that this was Mae's room.

He turned, but Mae was staring at the hallway. She looked in both directions, and even towards the ceiling. Then she followed him inside and closed the door. With a finger to her lips, she walked over to her closet, motioning for him to follow. He did, mostly because he was speechless at her strange behavior. She pushed a pile of sheets and a pillow into his arms and started shoving aside hangers. As the clothes parted, he saw a door. She opened it. He half-expected a snow-covered forest to be on the other side, but there was just a staircase.

"I put a flashlight in the pillowcase," Mae whispered. "Now go. No one knows about this place."

"Wait, what? I'm not leaving?"

"Shh! No. I'm still working on that."

"But you said my dad—"

"I don't even have his number. Listen, just go. The stairs are the only way into the attic. I'm going to lock my bedroom door. No one will be able to get in. It should work!" She looked into his eyes and did something he didn't expect. She grabbed him and hugged him tight, a rib-crushing hug. He could feel Hilde squirming against the embrace. Then Mae released him and pushed him behind the door. He was too shocked to do anything. The door closed with a soft click and he blinked a few times in the sudden darkness. With no other choice, he climbed the stairs. He came to a landing, but there was no door to the second floor. Just more stairs leading up. The air was warm and powdery, like bits of it had atrophied in the long disused space.

When he finally emerged into the attic proper, it was one long, dark room. Dusty cardboard boxes, cans of paint, old vacuums and any number of objects were piled along the walls. The only light came from a few square windows covered in spiderwebs. Garrison dropped the bedclothes and checked on Hilde. She meowed at him. He put her down on the blankets, gave her an ear scratch, and then headed over to a window. Shadowy figures ran along the driveway, away from the house. Guess there wouldn't be a resistance.

Garrison turned around and slid down the wall. Carly's journal bumped his spine, and he took it out.

It was small, about half the size of regular paper. The cover was thick, made of smooth leather dyed a dark teal. There was no name on the front, no cute words of encouragement. He only knew it was Carly's journal from the few times he saw it on her desk when he visited. He ran his hand over the cover, wondering what it would say inside. Would he find out that Carly was a traitor? He prayed with every cell of his being that wasn't the case and opened the book.

Day 162, Year 18, Century 21

I feel silly, horrible, and sore. My muscles ache. There is a ringing in my ears and I don't know who I am. How can that be? I can remember how to write, talk and that I love these small fried pastries with cinnamon and sugar, but not who I am or how I got here.

The healer says it's normal. She claims my memory will return in time. She thinks writing my thoughts down here will help. I'm not so sure. When I try to recall anything, it slips away, leaving me empty. Sometimes if I don't try, if I lay down and relax, images come. Memories, perhaps? The problem is they are disjointed and terrifying. I see a man with a deer's head who wants my blood. I don't know why, and I don't know if the deer head is a mask or a figment of my imagination, but it makes my heart race and my skin prickle. My memories seem to have teeth and claws. Maybe I don't want to remember.

Garrison frowned. Clearly, Carly didn't remember her life before. And did the deer dude really want her blood? He hoped that was just a figment of Carly's messed-up head, because...yuck. And what did he want it for? Picturing

Devose's creepy half-animal body made Garrison shiver. How did he get that way?

Garrison also noted the odd way she wrote the date, although it was probably the least strange thing about the whole journal entry. She arrived on June 11. Therefore, that must be the 162nd day of the year. Interesting. He turned a few pages.

Day 164, Year 18 Century 21

I have nowhere to turn. Paul, as they call him, came to my room. He threatened me and it unlocked some memories. Horrible ones. I'm treacherous — engaged to the lord of darkness, living in his house, eating his food. And I didn't care. Not until he wanted to marry me, the same day as my mother's funeral. I refused, and he beat me. Sune stole me away, convinced me to transform into a bird. I can do that, transform into any animal I want. It's how I crossed the boundary to the farm, I think. I can almost remember.

Perhaps I should become something tiny and sneak under the door. But then where would I go? Devose's mercenaries are everywhere. There is no safe place. Except here. The farm.

No one here can ever find out who I am. How I got across the boundary. They would exile me and send me back to my doom.

Garrison blinked rapidly. Paul threatened Carly? She's engaged to Devose? And she lives with him? Not to mention that she can turn into an animal? What next?

Although, the transforming thing would explain how she got out of her room. If she turned into something small and went under the door. Did her clothes change with her? The dress on the floor of her room seemed to be the answer. So, she would have been naked tonight. Garrison felt his face go red, thinking about Carly that way in his room, as she got clothes from his dresser.

And who the heck was Sune?

He flipped to the last entry. It was just a day later.

Day 165, Year 18, Century 21

Everything's gone wrong. Garrison didn't like my fumsup even though I worked all night on it. And we got into a terrible fight. He wanted to know how I got through the boundary, but I can't tell him! Shapeshifters are despised. The others here would turn on me, get me sent away. Even if Garrison kept it a secret, there is still Paul. If he found out I told, he'd expose my connection to Devose. I'd be condemned. Oh, Garrison. Why couldn't you just leave it all alone?

Garrison winced. He suddenly felt like a jerk. She had good reason to be scared. The half-deer lord of darkness wanted to marry her, even though she was a kid, and then decided to beat her senseless when she didn't go along with it. And he may or may not want her blood. Garrison still wasn't clear on that. He closed his eyes, remembering the day they found Carly. Was it really less than a week ago? He saw the bruises in his mind. He felt his lip curl. "Monster," he whispered. Yet, she went back. Offered herself up as a sacrifice. Why? To save him?

Something bumped against his knee. He opened his eyes to see Hilde there. As tears slid down his cheeks, she began to purr and rub his ankle. He reached out to pet her head. "At least I could save you."

After a few minutes, he got up to make a proper bed. As proper as he could on the floor. He spread out a thin white sheet beneath a window. He piled the pillows on one side and finally added a soft blanket on top. When Garrison lay down, Hilde immediately curled into his side. He smiled at her, an ache in his chest that was both happy and sad. His mind kept returning to Carly alone in the night with Devose. Was she being bled dry? Was she married? He didn't want to imagine any of it, but his consciousness was a pinball bouncing around the scenes of a horror movie.

CHAPTER 29

Carly sat stiffly in her chair. She wasn't tied up, which was a good sign. But she had a guard. He sat sideways in front of the door of the canvas tent, where he could watch both her and the action in camp. There was a lot of action. Dark figures, with weapons hanging from their belts and shoulders, walked ceaselessly around. She saw them pass the open flap and heard their weapons jangle. She could shift, turn into an animal and escape. It was tempting. No one in camp could fly, so they'd never be able to catch her. But she wouldn't do it. She went with Devose, willingly, because the moment he threatened Mae and Garrison, she knew she couldn't just leave and let them get hurt. So, she struck her bargain with him, and she would be true to her word.

The guard at the tent door moved, bringing her back to the present. She tried engaging the guard in conversation, but he ignored her. She tried asking for water. He ignored that, too. She gave up and stared outside. Deep down, she realized she hoped to see Sune. To know he was alright. She knew he wouldn't come to her, not with the guard here. Their friendship was secret. He told her once that his father, Devose, forbade him from even entering her wing. Sune ignored him, of course, sneaking around the outside of the large house to visit her. She remembered spotting him that first time, concealed in a maple tree. They were roughly the same age, and she was lonely in the big house, especially because as her mother got more involved with Devose, the less Carly saw of her. Carly assumed it was because Devose was wooing her. Her mother would visit him and come back very late, exhausted. Now Carly realized that her mother was sacrificing her blood all that time.

Carly's body shuddered, pimpled flesh appearing on her arms. She was afraid of the bloodletting. Would it hurt? Well, of course it would hurt. Her heart sped up and her breathing became more like gasps. She glanced at the guard. Still no reaction.

She closed her eyes and forced herself to breathe deeply. Fear wouldn't help her through this. Devose wasn't here yet. She still had time.

When she opened her eyes, he was standing there. His stag head cocked to the side in consideration. "Carly, my dear. What are you doing?"

She looked at her lap. "Nothing."

"Liar. I can hear your heart racing. Do not worry, my dear. It is not nearly as bad as you imagine." He turned to the guard. "You may leave us."

The guard barely nodded before calmly walking through the door. Devose turned to close the flap, tying it shut.

Carly tried to swallow, but her mouth was dry. The two small lanterns lit the interior with a soft yellow glow that was too...too...intimate. She squirmed. She couldn't help it.

Devose took the guards' chair and moved it close to hers. When he grinned at her, she realized she was leaning away from him. She forced herself to sit straight.

"It's true, I do love a deep primal fear," he said, in a breathy voice that brought the gooseflesh out more. "However, you need not fear me. I merely want some of your blood."

Carly tried to speak. It didn't work.

Devose sat on the edge of his chair, too close. She could feel the heat from his body. She closed her hands into fists. "You wanted to marry me."

"Ah, that. Yes. I did. Well, I did, and I didn't. You see, your mother's blood wasn't quite enough. Over the years, it transformed me bit by bit from that awful deer shape the Fotismeno trapped me inside." He sneered, glancing at the ring on his left hand.

Carly glanced at it, too. It was a gold man's ring, with some kind of design on the top. Sune told her Devose was looking for a ring. The Fotismeno's ring. Was that it? Devose took her arm in his hand. Her muscles instantly went rigid.

"Okay, I do love it. Your fear." He practically laughed.

She hated him.

He pushed the shawl she was wearing over her shirt up and turned her arm to expose the underside. He ran a long, tan finger over the veins. "Shapeshifters are so rare," he whispered. "Nearly myth. It took me centuries to find your mother. And then, by some great fortune, she also had a daughter. But with you, the line ends. Unless," he used the edges of his nail to caress her skin, "you have a child."

She jerked her hand away. She couldn't help it.

He actually did laugh then.

"No!" she said.

"Be still. Tonight, I only want what you're willing to give. There is plenty of time for the rest."

"But last time..." she trailed off, unable to finish the sentence.

He shrugged. "I was, shall we say, annoyed that night. I'd just lost your mother and was still half beast." He snarled the word.

Carly imagined how it must chafe his vain nature. He was forever having new suits tailored to his changing body, shoes polished to a mirror shine, solid gold cufflinks, and tie chains. Once upon a time, she felt sorry for him, forced to be part animal. But not now. Now, it seemed like a fitting punishment.

"I wanted to continue your line, keep a shifter in the family. Just in case. That was always the intention when you were older. However, that night, I felt compelled to advance my plans. It was a mistake, as it turned out. Forced you to run away." He smiled at her. "Clever, going to the Wagon Wheel. I didn't know shifters could pass through the boundary. I assume you managed it in animal form?"

Carly didn't answer.

"Oh, child. Shall we just get it over with?"

"What if I change my mind?"

Devose stopped smiling. She saw his jaw clench and the smell of animal hide was stronger. Muscles along his neck tensed. Then he relaxed into the chair again. "Then I would take torches and burn that farmhouse to the ground. With everyone inside."

Carly swallowed, trying to unsee the image of Garrison burning alive. "Okay," she said. She put her arm back down, not quite in his hands, but near enough that he understood. "I'm ready." The last words were more of a breath than actual words.

Devose smiled again, and Carly looked away. She heard something, an object being removed from a pocket, but she refused to look. He said something to her, but she wasn't listening. She squeezed her eyes tight and forced her mind to go blank.

Something touched her skin, but there was no pain. Then he squeezed her arm gently, and she felt the skin part. She felt the blood push to the surface. The knife must have been very sharp. The pain was there, but minor, like a paper cut. She opened her eyes and saw her wrist drenched in red. It dripped down on both sides, landing in a large, shallow bowl.

The sight made her dizzy, and her body seemed to waver.

"Careful. We can't have any wasted."

She swallowed and closed her eyes. She thought about flying, about Sune, about Garrison, only coming back to herself when she felt him tie something around her wrist. It was a strip of cloth. The red blood was already beginning to weep through.

"The binding was infused with an ointment to promote clotting. The bleeding will stop soon." He took the bowl and sniffed it. "It's so clean. So pure." He tilted his animal head back and drank, like it was soup. Carly's stomach turned inside out. She felt herself slip into sleep. Strange, she hadn't been at all tired before.

***

When Carly woke, Devose was still in the tent. He was talking to another man. She recognized his companion. Maras. Part butler, part second in command, Maras was a simpering little man who resembled a frog. He glared at everyone with bulging eyes, full of arrogance at being in Devose's inner circle.

"It's a crown, sir," Maras was saying. "A crown befitting a king."

Devose tilted his head this way and that in the mirror Maras was holding. "I suppose it is rather like a crown."

Carly squinted. The mirror's surface was turned towards her, and she saw Devose's reflection. His skin was a deep tan, shadowed around the chin with stubble. His nose was long and wide. Above it, his eyes were solid black, a bit more deer than man. Brown hair covered his scalp. And antlers rose from it, curved into each other. It looked a bit like a crown. Or devil horns. She closed her eyes again.

Footsteps told her someone else entered the tent. "The team is assembled, sir," came a voice a few seconds afterwards.

"Wonderful," Devose replied. "Place your decoy right by the opening. The rest should be hidden out of sight."

"Yes, sir."

"And Hog. There can be no mistakes. I want the silver-eyed boy brought to me."

Carly gasped. She hadn't meant to, but when she realized they were talking about Garrison, it just escaped. She opened her eyes. The men were staring at her. She bit her lip and shook her head.

Devose laughed. "You can't have it both ways, my dear. After all, you did make a deal with the devil." Devose gave a signal, and the men left, Maras giving her the stink eye.

She sat up. She would leave, she decided. Warn Garrison, and then run away somewhere Devose couldn't find her. She would live off berries and nuts if she had to. She thought of Sune then, of all that he risked for her, and hoped she could say goodbye. Maybe he was in the camp.

She stood up, her legs shakier than she expected. Probably just the aftereffects of adrenaline, she thought. Her heart was pounding, too. She imagined going small, a bird. They were her favorite.

She imagined her arms becoming wings, and her soft feet shrinking to sharp, hard talons.

Something wasn't right.

She opened her eyes and looked down. She was herself, standing there in Garrison's cotton shirt and denim pants.

There wasn't even a single feather on her skin. What was wrong? What happened?

The blood! She realized in a rush. The blood Devose took was her power! Would it come back? Or had she given it away forever?

She crashed onto the cot, sobs tearing her chest apart.

CHAPTER 30

Garrison woke to sunlight streaming through the small attic windows. His eyes were crusty and he rubbed at them. A knock came at the stairs door, two soft and one hard. Getting up, Garrison heard the door open, and then shut, quickly. He went over and peered down. It was dark in the staircase, but if he craned his neck to look past the landing, he could see the outline of a food tray. He ran to the bottom of the steps greedily, carrying the tray back to his makeshift bed. There was a bowl of cat food and breakfast for him. A note with his name on it was on one side. He unfolded it.

Garrison,

I am sorry about this. I just can't stand the idea of him getting you. And he won't give up if he thinks you're still here. Stay hidden and stay quiet. Use the bathroom in my room if you need. My bedroom door will be locked, so no one can get in. I'll bring more food later. I already grabbed Hilde's litter box. Take it into the attic with you today.

I'll get you out of this. I swear. I (a word was scribbled out) *hope you forgive me.*

~ Mae

Was he really just supposed to hide here while Devose ruined everything? He munched on an English muffin. Carly was in serious trouble and Mae was being threatened with...well, it sounded like death. He felt so helpless.

He stood up to look out the window. There was no one outside, not even Mae doing chores.

What would happen once Devose took the house? Could he turn the protection against them? Would it be a safe place for evil?

A soft scraping halted his pessimistic thought spiral. It was in the vicinity of the stairs. Mae knocked, so he knew it wasn't her. Garrison looked around. There was a heavy-looking black and silver candlestick on top of an old coffee table. He ran over to it, trying not to make any noise. Maybe it was Paul. Or worse, Devose. He held the candlestick like a baseball bat and crept towards the stairs.

The door at the bottom was just opening when he reached it, light spilling into the space. Garrison took a shaky breath, holding the candlestick higher. Someone entered, then reclosed the door. In the gloom, Garrison could only see a black shape. It didn't move, and neither did Garrison.

"For goodness' sake, put that down. You're making me itch."

It was Tuck.

Garrison lowered the candlestick. Tuck came up the stairs, eyeing Garrison's makeshift bat as though it were a poisonous insect.

"What is it?" asked Garrison.

"It's silver."

"No. It's a candlestick."

Tuck rolled his eyes. "It's made of silver, idiot."

"So?"

"So, we're allergic to it."

"Wait, what?"

Tuck stepped around Garrison into the attic proper.

Garrison walked after him.

"Seriously. Put it down. Over there." Tuck waved to the far corner. "Way over there. I feel itchy all over." Garrison did so. When he turned back, Tuck was bent, looking out the window.

"Not much of a view," he said.

"What do you mean, you're allergic to it?"

"I suppose it's best if you know." Tuck turned around and crossed his arms. "It hurts us. Being near it long enough will cause a rash to break out. Touching it directly will break open our skin."

"Silver can kill you?"

"I suppose," said Tuck, uncrossing his arms and turning away. "It injures us, certainly."

"That's why Mae removed her bracelet when Devose came."

"Indeed."

"But she never got a chance to use it because Carly gave herself up."

Tuck gave him an eyebrow raise he knew was skepticism.

"Here, I can prove it." Garrison pulled the journal from beneath a fold in the blanket.

"Well, look who has sticky fingers."

"Just read it."

Tuck took it and opened the pages.

"By the way," Garrison asked. "How did you know I was up here?"

Tuck looked at him. "I know every inch of this house. That didn't change just because Mae remodeled to make a suite. It was the obvious choice."

"But didn't Mae lock her door?"

Tuck grinned, turning back to the journal.

Garrison looked at Tuck's pocket. He could just make out the subtle outline of Tuck's lock picks. Tuck truly was his hero.

Unfortunately, his hero soon became ill. Garrison saw Tuck's face change as he read more of Carly's journal. It went from playful to serious. Then, all the color drained completely. "Paul's the spy? Impossible. He's been coming and going for the past month. He had a missive from the queen." Tuck began pacing. "Although, at the time, I did think it strange I wasn't sent to deliver it. I thought maybe she forgot about me. Hoped, really."

"He spied on us, stole my mom's map and threatened Carly. He's going down."

Tuck rolled his eyes on the other side of the attic. "Noble sentiment, Romeo. However, it doesn't change facts. Devose can get onto the grounds. Into the house whenever he wants. If we want to know how, and stop him, we need to know what your mom hid in those woods. What he has."

Garrison thought for a moment. "We could email her."

Tuck turned around, excited. "Yes! Come on."

"No way. If Mae catches me, she'll freak. I'll give you my mom's email address..."

Tuck was shaking his head. "Won't work."

"Why not?"

"Because I can't use the computer."

"What?"

"Technology like that doesn't exist in my world. If I try to touch it, it will explode, or at the very least, stop working. Sometimes I can't touch it at all."

Garrison could feel his mouth hanging open. "You don't have computers?"

Tuck shook his head once.

"Or email?"

Another head shake.

"Phones?"

"Not the kind you carry around in your pocket," Tuck said.

"I just don't believe it. You can break through the layers of the world, change into animals, and mind-control humans, but you haven't invented the cell phone?"

"That is a bit of an oversimplification, but, in the interest of time, fine. Yes. As to technology, let's just say that our world took a different path early in the Industrial Revolution. Most of the mechanical devices work on steam or simple batteries. We have electricity, but no circuit thingies."

"Circuit thingies are not a thing."

Tuck shrugged. "The point is, you have to do the emailing. If I try, it will stop working." He walked over to the steps and headed down. Garrison reluctantly followed.

"But how do you know? Have you ever tried?" Garrison asked at the landing.

Tuck stopped on the floor below, his hand on the doorknob. "Yes, I've tried."

"When? I mean, when was the last time? Maybe things are different now."

"I tried five days ago." Tuck turned the knob and the door opened.

"Wait," Garrison said as they entered Mae's empty bedroom. "I was here 5 days ago."

"This way," Tuck said, ignoring him.

Garrison was thinking through the events. That was the day before Carly arrived, before he went to town for a new charger. The day his game quit working. He stopped. "You killed my video game?"

"I didn't mean to. I just wanted to try it. Now, come on, the computer is in here."

Garrison didn't know whether to believe Tuck or not. It was hard to tell when he was being sincere.

A thought popped into his head. What would have happened if Tuck never touched his game? Would Garrison have stayed in his room? Alone? Never meeting Carly? Or saving Hilde? Finding the map? Becoming friends with Tuck? He saw a version of himself in his mind, relaxing on the bed, head bent over the small screen. He mashed buttons and reveled in the game's catchy action music. People ran around outside the bedroom window. Smoke erupted from the trees. But the Garrison on the bed didn't even notice. The hypothetical image made him feel hollow inside. Hollow and cold.

Shaking off the alternative present, Garrison followed Tuck into a small office off the main room. He took one look at the desk and gasped. "Mae has an Alienware Aurora R7? That's a gaming computer!"

"She says it's the fastest computer she's ever had."

Garrison ran his hand up the side. "This is unbelievable."

"Fall in love later. We need to hurry. I'll keep a lookout."

Garrison shook the mouse, and the computer instantly lit up. Luckily, Mae didn't use a password. It took him just a few seconds to find Mae's email and open it. There was an unread message from his mom in bold. He double clicked it.

Hi, Mom,

Thanks for the update on Garrison. His message a few days ago sounded so sad; I was worried. He's been a loner since, well, since before the divorce, if I'm being honest. Almost pushes people away and hides himself in those pointless games. I worry about him. Please tell him I miss him.

Everything here is great. Nice colleagues with all kinds of stories about travel. Plus, it feels so gratifying to help people who need it. I just hope—

Tuck interrupted. "Shoot. Here she comes. Hide!"

Garrison slid under the desk, hitting the sleep button on the keyboard on the way down.

He heard the door open to the bedroom. Footsteps coming closer. Garrison shut his eyes and held his breath. His heart rammed itself against his ribs. What if Mae went upstairs to check on him? He grimaced. She would see that he wasn't there. What would she think? What would she do?

The footsteps receded. Then Tuck said, "Okay. The coast is clear."

Garrison slid out from under the desk in time to see Tuck emerge from behind Mae's open bathroom door. "What is taking so long?" Tuck asked.

Ah, nothing, Garrison thought, just having a panic attack over here. Without reading the rest of his mother's email, he hit reply.

"Hi, Mom," he wrote, then deleted it. "Hi, Rachel. Glad you are having a good time. I have a question. What did you hide in the woods when you were little? You made a treasure map to it. Garrison found it and we were just wondering. "

Garrison read it back over. He wasn't sure it sounded like Mae, but he didn't have time to worry about it. He hit send. Then he went into the sent folder and deleted the email. He also marked his mom's message as unread. He hoped that would be enough to prevent Mae from catching on. "Okay, it's done," he said to Tuck.

"Good."

"What do we do now?"

Tuck sighed. "Unfortunately, now we wait. You head back upstairs. I need to go have a conversation with Mae." He tapped Carly's journal against his chest.

"You're not giving her that, are you?"

"It's the only way to convince her about Paul."

Garrison grimaced. He didn't like it, but he thought Tuck might be right. Mae certainly wouldn't just take his word for it. Paul seemed so nice.

"Here," Tuck said, handing Garrison a deck of cards that materialized from somewhere.

"What am I supposed to do with these?"

Tuck rolled his eyes and left. Garrison climbed back up into the attic.

The rest of the day passed slower than any other Garrison spent at the Wagon Wheel Farm. Mae delivered lunch at about noon and told him Paul had escaped. They went to his room immediately after Tuck showed her the journal, but he was already gone.

Garrison suggested he go back to his own room then, since there was no more spy. Mae shook her head. She said it was better to be out of sight.

As it happened, *out of sight* doubled for boring. Garrison stared out the window at the leaves swaying in the slight breeze and listened to the sound of cicadas. There wasn't even a radio up here. It gave him plenty of time to worry.

What if Mae got the email from his mom first? Would she figure out he sent it? He snuck down the stairs when he knew she would be making dinner to check. Nothing.

Returning to the attic, he took out the cards Tuck gave him and tried a game of solitaire. Since he only ever played it online, he wasn't sure he was doing it correctly, but it passed the time.

When the sun finally set, Garrison lay down and closed his eyes, hoping sleep would make the time go more quickly. It did not. Instead of sleeping, he watched as a shaft of moonlight moved slowly up the angled ceiling until it disappeared. Hilde was a warm spot on the back of his knee. He missed his bed. He missed Tuck and playing pranks and dinner with everyone together and visiting Carly. Deeper still, he felt an ache for his mom. Hilde yawned with her tiny fang teeth and circled three times. At least she wasn't having a hard time sleeping.

Very early the next day, he went down the stairs to Mae's bedroom door. His stomach in knots, he silently prayed Mae didn't check her email first thing in the morning. He knocked softly at the door, two soft and one hard, because the last thing he wanted was to catch Mae getting dressed.

He heard footsteps, and Mae opened the door a crack. "I need to use the bathroom," Garrison whispered, "Didn't want to scare you."

She opened the door fully. "I need to start breakfast," she whispered back, "or they'll know something is up."

Garrison nodded, trying not to look relieved. She must not have seen an unexpected email.

When Mae left, he snuck into her office. No new emails from his mom. Blast! Garrison returned to the attic, wishing Tuck would come visit him.

In the afternoon, Garrison got another chance to check Mae's emails while she was outside doing chores. After all the waiting, bold text never looked so good. He clicked on it.

I can't believe you still have that map! Wow! I think I hid a bunch of random stuff I found in the woods. At the time, I considered it all to be treasures. There were some bird feathers, I think, and interesting stones. An old can. Oh, and a ring — a huge ugly thing that must have been dropped a long time ago. Gosh. I wonder if all that stuff is still there.

By the way, I never asked you. How are the chickens doing? Is their sickness any better?

Garrison stopped reading and deleted the email before heading back up the stairs. Had Devose been wearing a ring the other night? Garrison tried to remember. He pictured the black suit. Devose's hands were mostly in his pockets, except for once. Gloves! He was wearing gloves. Garrison sat down with a huff.

When Tuck finally came, Garrison started talking first. "Mom answered. She hid a bunch of stuff, most of it boring, but one thing was a ring. An old one she found in the woods. Could that be it?"

Tuck leaned against a dusty dresser as though he were exhausted. "No idea."

"It's gotta be. Devose was wearing gloves the other night. And unless it's a magic feather, and this is Dumbo…" Garrison trailed off when he noticed Tuck's expression. "What's wrong?"

Tuck's jaw clenched and unclenched before he answered. "The queen is shutting down the portal. No one will be allowed through here anymore. And I'm being recalled to court. Permanently."

"You're leaving?"

Tuck looked away. "I have to."

Garrison struggled for words. He thought the ring would be good news. That Tuck would have a plan to fix things. "What about Sam and Rebecca? Mae?"

"Mae plans to stay. She says it's to protect this place. She thinks because it's just Devose who can cross and not his mercenaries, she's got a shot. I don't know. What if he can bring people, though? Either way, the queen is declaring this place unsafe. She's giving it up to the dark side." Tuck gave Garrison a sideways look. "Sorry."

Garrison didn't know if the apology was for the queen giving up or for explaining that Mae was going to make a stand against Devose. Garrison shivered.

"Anyway," Tuck went on. "I think it has more to do with distracting Devose."

That caught Garrison's attention. "Distract him from what?"

Tuck looked at Garrison and raised an eyebrow.

Garrison's worst fear was confirmed. "Me?"

Tuck nodded. "If he's busy trying to get to her, you can get away. He doesn't know where you live. You're a needle in a haystack, just like you were before you came. Sam and Rebecca plan to stay too." Tuck looked jealous, despite the obvious threat this meant to their lives.

"This can't be happening," Garrison said, stomping across the attic, kicking at boxes. Hilde ran after a dust bunny. Garrison envied her naivety. "All this because of a kid's map? And a stupid old ring?"

"Quite. Especially considering...." Tuck stopped.

"Considering what?"

"Considering that your mother is unable to see us."

"So?"

"Your mother can't see us!"

"You said that already."

Tuck started smiling, a manic variety that set Garrison on edge. "She can't see things that exist only in our realm. Therefore, the ring must be from the human realm. Mae can get it."

Garrison furrowed his brow. "But Devose has it." It was too late, however. Tuck was already rushing down the stairs. Garrison followed him.

"Stay here for a minute," Tuck said to him as they entered Mae's room. "I'll be right back." With that, Tuck vanished into the hallway.

When Tuck returned, Mae was with him. She didn't sound happy. "I don't know what is so urgent. I'm trying to help Sam and Rebecca fortify their room."

"Mae," Tuck said, shutting the door. "Garrison found out what Rachel hid. It was a ring."

Mae looked at Garrison. Her eyes narrowed, and she looked over at her office, no doubt guessing how he managed it. His cheeks felt hot.

"It doesn't matter what it is. It lets him into the boundary. This place is no longer protected."

"But you can go get it."

"Impossible."

"No, listen," argued Tuck. Garrison never heard this shaky edge in Tuck's voice. It sounded desperate. "If Rachel found it in the woods, like she said, then it still resides in the human realm. What Devose has is only a copy!"

Mae shook her head and opened her mouth, but Tuck talked over her. "It's true. I know about this stuff. Rachel saw it. Touched it. But she can't see or feel us, not even in the house. So it must be a human-made object. Okay, so if that's true, Devose could only have used his power to copy it. He can't touch items in the human world. None of us can. But he's so powerful, he could use some of that power to replicate a human object. I'm willing to bet that's what he did. But the original ring is still here. The human realm. That means you can go get it and use its power too. It's connected to the boundary, so you can use it to stop Devose crossing. Ward him off. Maybe reinforce the protection."

Mae took a deep breath and blew it out. "Tuck...I know how much this place means to you."

Tuck glanced at Garrison, shuffling his feet. "It's not that."

"Let's assume what you say is true," Mae went on. "I'd have to go where Rachel hid the ring and we—"

"Know where that is," interrupted Garrison. "Devose dropped the map, remember?"

Mae gave him a look. "Exactly," she replied. "He dropped the map. It's a trap. Just like I said before. This changes nothing."

"But…"

"All you have are guesses. We don't even know for sure this ring has anything to do with Devose getting through." Mae looked over at Garrison. "There's too much at stake for me to run off on a desperate hope."

Neither Garrison nor Tuck said anything.

Mae continued in a softer voice, "I suggest you get on with your goodbye. Once I line my door with silver, Tuck won't be able to sneak in anymore. Lock picks or no lock picks."

Silence filled the space. Mae pressed her lips together and left.

"So. After this is all over, you'll visit, right?" Garrison asked.

"I'm sorry, Garrison."

Garrison knew that meant no. He looked out Mae's glass doors, trying to calm his emotions. He really, really, didn't want to cry. The grass waved in the breeze. He could almost smell the farm air through the window. A thought occurred to him. "Why do you think Mae can use the power of the ring against Devose?"

Tuck took a moment to answer. "If you hadn't noticed, your grandmother is not like most of your kind." His voice was very sarcastic. Garrison ignored it.

"For real, why?"

"Not now, Garrison."

"It doesn't sound like there will be a later."

Tuck rubbed his face. "Well, for starters, she can see us. She has the power to bring people into the portal. We think one of her ancestors helped the queen defeat Devose."

"Like in the legend?"

Tuck nodded. "It has to be."

"Okay. So, you're saying Mae's special. She's got the same genes as someone who beat Devose a long time ago. And you think those genes can control the ring that's here, the one in my world?"

"Yes. Because the copy is only in my—"

"So it's in my genes, too?"

Tuck just stared at him.

"I'm her grandson. I can see you. I can get people through the boundary."

"It's risky."

Garrison thought about it, thought about what it would mean. It was strange, because a week ago, he wanted to leave. Any reason for being sent home would have been welcome. But now, he felt differently. This place, with its warm meals and country smells. He thought of Mae's commanding presence, Sam's solid one and the mothering coos of Rebecca. This place had changed him. He wanted to be here. He looked at Tuck. "This is my home. I'll do anything to protect it."

Tuck watched him for a moment, probably recognizing words he once said to Garrison. He nodded.

"We'll need my mom's map," Garrison said.

Tuck put up his hand, showing his palm. Then he closed his fingers. When he opened them, there lay a familiar piece of folded paper.

"You had that the whole time?" Garrison asked.

"Maybe."

Garrison took the map and unfolded it. He could see the house, the barn, the garden, the firepit, etc. He read the text at the bottom. "From lioness...uh...*be you*?"

"Beau isn't pronounced like that. It's pronounced like *bow*. It means a man you're courting."

Garrison just stared at him.

"I suppose you would say boyfriend."

"Okay," Garrison said, his eyes doing a small roll, "so from the lioness' boyfriend, there are three dancing pine trees. Whatever that means. But at least the lion is a starting point." He pointed to her drawing. It was a scribbled lion face.

"That is hardly a starting point," said Tuck, looking at the map over Garrison's shoulder. "That's a statue somewhere west of the house, in the middle of a forest of trees. And quite possibly enemy territory."

"We don't know it's enemy territory."

"Yes, we do. Mae was right about why Devose gave us back the map."

"He could have dropped it. Accidentally."

Tuck rolled his eyes. "It's definitely a trap."

"Do we have a choice?"

"No. Now come on. We should get you some weapons."

Garrison followed him back to the attic.

CHAPTER 31

When Tuck mentioned weapons, Garrison pictured a sword, as unrealistic as that might have been. A knife or an axe might have made more sense, since they were on a farm. In reality, the weapons were none of those things. Tuck led Garrison to a bunch of junk in the attic and started sniffing at boxes like a bloodhound.

"What are you doing?"

"Shhh." He moved to another area of the attic and held out his hand. "Okay, here. Open that."

Garrison shrugged and pulled on the lid of a shallow box. It sprang open, revealing dull-looking forks, knives and spoons. "You're kidding."

Tuck crossed his arms. "They're silver and they're portable," he said, a bit defensively. "Now, grab a couple and put them along your left wrist. We can tie them on with this."

"Is that a shoelace?" Garrison asked.

Tuck grinned.

He wound the cord around the silverware. Garrison noticed he was being very careful that his fingers didn't actually touch the utensils. He also grimaced the entire time.

"There." Tuck stepped back. "It's like a knight's vambrace."

"A what?"

Tuck huffed. "From a suit of armor? A vambrace protects the forearm."

Garrison looked down at his forearm. The fork tines stuck out unevenly under the shoelace. He twisted his wrist to see the section with butter knives, but it wasn't much better. "I look ridiculous."

"I'll go pack up some supplies and meet you in Mae's room as soon as she leaves tomorrow."

"Wait. Tomorrow? Why not now?"

"Because it's getting dark. Devose's minions are stronger at night. Haven't you ever noticed that all your fears seem bigger in the dark?"

Garrison shrugged, but he had. He remembered, as a little boy, hiding under the covers, certain some unseen terror was out there, waiting for him. The monster under the bed, the axe murderer lurking in the closet, the man with the droopy eyes from the news report on a child molester.

"We'll stand a better chance of succeeding with daylight on our side," Tuck was saying. "Now put a long sleeve shirt on. You look ridiculous."

Garrison glared at him, but it did no good. He was already gone, a slight laugh lingering in the air.

Garrison examined his homemade vambrace again. Experimentally, he pulled a fork out and brandished it like a sword. The other utensils all fell to the floor. "Perfect. Just perfect." He sighed.

Very early the next morning, Garrison was dreaming. He was on a field, a soccer ball at his feet. He was moving and standing still at the same time, like the other players were in slow motion — dark shapes with no faces. Everyone was counting on him to score. Pulling his foot back, he paused, uncertain.

He wouldn't make it. He had no friends. He wasn't important.

Gritting his teeth, he moved, propelling his foot forward to connect with the ball. It cracked, shattering into a million pieces. He was so startled that he sat up, fully awake. There was broken glass on the floor a few feet away. Tuck was standing just inside, wrapping a cloth around his fist. Hilde was hiding across the room between two boxes, her tail huge.

Garrison turned back to Tuck. "What did you do?"

"Mae already lined the place with silver. I couldn't get in any other way."

Garrison walked over to the broken window and looked down. "We're three stories up."

Tuck brushed his knuckles on his breast like there was a badge there. He looked smug. "I'm a good climber."

Garrison looked down again. There wasn't even a drain pipe. "Well, I'm not a good climber, so how do you propose we get out?"

"You'll go through the door."

Garrison suddenly felt uneasy. He stalled. "Mae is going to kill you, you know. For breaking that window."

Tuck spoke so softly when he answered that Garrison almost missed it. "Honestly, if we don't get that ring back, I'd welcome it."

Garrison opened his mouth to ask what Tuck meant, but Tuck spoke again, louder. "Mae's in the kitchen, making coffee right now. After she brings you breakfast, head downstairs and out the French doors — don't go through the house. Stick to the shadows and make your way to the front porch. I'll meet you out front. DON'T LET ANYONE SEE YOU."

Tuck turned away.

Garrison called out. "Wait, the vambrace. I need you to retie it."

"Honestly."

Garrison held it in place, so Tuck didn't have to touch the metal. Last night, Garrison made slip knots for each utensil handle. It was harder to get them out quickly, but at least when he took one out, they didn't all fall out.

Tuck tied a fast bow, then reached out the window. He pulled himself through it without touching a single shard. It was amazing. Garrison looked down to watch him spread himself across a small piece of siding that formed a ledge. It wasn't more than 3 inches deep. Then he was at the junction of the roof to the balcony below. A small drop and Tuck was using the railing like a jungle gym, swinging across to the gutter on the far side. There was a prickly heat across Garrison's neck and face, which he suspected was a mixture of jealousy and awe.

Mae came 30 minutes later. Her special knock nearly sent him into a panic attack. He jerked involuntarily, disturbing Hilde asleep on his lap. After the door closed, he went to grab the tray. He wolfed down the food, not even really aware of what it was. He knew it was time to go. Still, he sat there. Did he really want to do this? A tug-o-war began in his chest — chivalry versus the unknown. He really wasn't sure which he wanted to win. He looked out the window. It wasn't early morning anymore. The sun was brighter. He shot up. Tuck would be waiting for him. Probably wondering where he was. He grabbed Hilde and her litter box, then tiptoed downstairs. He couldn't leave her in the attic while he was gone. The window was broken. She might get out.

Garrison didn't knock at the door, but opened it and peeked out into Mae's room. She wasn't there. The French doors were just feet away. He put the litter box and Hilde down at the edge of the closet. Then he went back to shut the door to the attic very firmly. One more deep breath to stop his heart beating right through his chest, and he turned to make his way slowly across the carpet.

He heard something in the hall the moment he touched the handle to one of the French doors. He froze. What if Mae walked in and saw him? What would she do?

"No, no, Mae. It's enough," said Sam, his voice trailing away immediately.

Garrison sighed. He turned the door handle. It went down silently, and the door popped open a fraction of an inch. Garrison felt that his heart might burst. He swung open the door like it was booby trapped. When it was wide enough, he stepped through and closed it slowly behind him. There was no sound louder than a soft snick.

His attention was caught by an unusual glint. Small silver chains were wedged into the door frames on the outside. Garrison ran his finger against one, wondering if he would feel anything. An electric shock maybe, like a cow fence.

Nothing. It made him feel dumb. He flattened himself against the side of the house and moved towards the front porch.

He came up to the window of his old bedroom and glanced inside. Empty. Still mauve. There was something on the floor near the window that seemed out of place. A small dark something. He realized what it was in the next instant — the acorn action figure Carly gave him. How could he have thought she was a spy? He cringed. He stared at the little figure. His fingers twitched, ready to reach in and pluck it off the floor.

Garrison considered. The window was low to the ground. It wouldn't be too hard to open it and reach in for Carly's present. Then an image of Mae appeared. Her glowing eyes and huge stature bursting in on him, dragging him upstairs again. And locking him in this time. It was almost enough to make him forget the idea. Then he heard Carly's voice. "It will bring you luck." If ever he needed luck, it was today.

With a deep breath, he reached up and pushed on the sill. It made a soft scraping noise, but nothing compared to the groan he was expecting. He reached his arm in as far as it would go. His fingers brushed the small little man on the floor, but it wasn't enough. Garrison frowned. He pulled his arm back and pushed a bit more on the window. This time, it elicited a sound like Hilde being stepped on. It was too loud, too shrill to be ignored. Garrison leaned over the sill, grabbed the acorn man and ducked back down outside, leaving the window partially open.

Garrison didn't pause to see if anyone would come. His heart racing, he army-crawled forward a few feet, then stood and ran. He didn't stop until he hit something solid next to the front porch. It turned out to be Tuck, crouching next to a yew bush. "What took you so long?" he asked.

Garrison shook his head, trying to shake off the adrenaline. He pushed the acorn man into his pocket. "Nothing."

Tuck narrowed his eyes for a second and opened his mouth, but then closed it. He turned to scan their surroundings. "Wait here until I give the all clear."

"Sure. All clear. Yep. Completely understand—"

Tuck turned and glared. "Shhh!" Then he turned back and his demeanor altered before Garrison's eyes. His tight, worried features became a sly grin. His eyes glinted with mischief. He swaggered away from the house, calm and calculating.

It was so convincing, Garrison wondered which one was the real Tuck. He felt himself shiver.

Tuck circled in place once and then gave a slight jerk of his head. Garrison hesitated only a second before running to join him. Tuck matched his pace, and they raced towards the treeline — the edge of the farm's boundary. Tuck got there first and seemed to melt into the surroundings. Garrison paused just before stepping over. He came to a stop and looked back at the house. Mae walked out onto the side porch, the one closest to them. It was as though she knew someone was there. Garrison backed across the boundary, hugging a tree trunk to hide among the foliage. Mae scanned the yard, deep furrows visible across her forehead even at this distance. After a few moments, she went back inside.

Garrison turned to tell Tuck Mae was gone, but he was pulling off the gray felt satchel he was wearing off his shoulder. He took out some paper-wrapped sandwiches. Garrison's stomach growled as Tuck handed him one. After a few bites, Tuck brought out the map. He tapped the roaring lion's head. "Let's head west for a bit. Keep a lookout for anything that resembles a lion." Garrison nodded, hoping Tuck knew which way was west.

They walked single file, Tuck in front and Garrison following. He learned early on to keep his arms up to block the tiny branches on either side that slapped his face. They were everywhere, making him grit his teeth with each step. Garrison wasn't used to so much nature. Tuck, on the other hand, seemed just fine. He walked onward, arms casually at his sides. Were the branches even touching him?

A thought occurred to Garrison. "Tuck, are we in my world, or yours?"

Tuck didn't turn around. "You don't know?"

"Just answer."

"Interesting," Tuck muttered. "Yours. That's the one your mom was in when she hid the ring."

Something got past Garrison's guard and stung his left cheek. "Ow. So you don't feel these things. You can just walk through them."

"Pretty much."

Garrison could hear the smile in Tuck's voice. He glared at his back. "How are you even walking?"

Tuck shrugged. "There's still ground here in my world. That's probably why. I mean, where else would I go? Floating off into space?"

"Can you do that?"

Tuck looked over his shoulder in order to give Garrison a huge eye roll.

Garrison thought about how Tuck could scale the stories of Mae's house. "I think there's some truth to it."

Tuck shook his head.

"Okay, fine. But what about the house? How does that work? You touch the doors and even eat the food."

"The house and the surrounding property exist in both realms. The normal rules don't apply."

"The normal rules?" It came out very sarcastic.

"Fine. The standard rules of interaction. Nothing in your world can touch us and we can't touch it."

"But everything in the house is...touchable?"

"And everyone."

"What does that mean?"

"That means it's not just things, but people, too. In the human world, we typically can't touch you. Physically harm or affect anyone. But that's not true at the farm."

Garrison grimaced. "So that means Devose can hurt Mae."

"Yes. And also any human that comes to the house. Even if they can't see him."

Garrison rolled that idea around in his head. What would it be like to be in the farmhouse next to someone you couldn't see? Objects would move by unseen hands. Lights would go on and off. Again, he wondered if this was how the idea of ghosts began. The way he envisioned it, Tuck could easily be a poltergeist. Worse, if it was Devose. He would be attacking. Garrison felt the skin on his back ripple in a shiver, despite the heat.

Garrison looked down at the very narrow path of pressed grass and short plants they were following. There were no markers or signs around, just plants, trees, and bushes Garrison couldn't identify. He would never be able to find his way out of this place. How did Tuck even know this was west? "What happens if we get lost?"

"We won't," Tuck said. Then he paused, closing his eyes and tilting his head a little.

Garrison let his jaw drop. "Is that how your kind senses direction? Do you have a magnetic tracking system in your nose, like a bird or something?"

Tuck sighed loudly. "Of course not. I'm listening!"

"Oh." Garrison didn't know whether he was embarrassed or disappointed.

Tuck pulled out the map. "Look." He pointed to the house. "We ran straight west to the boundary. See the compass rose?" He pointed to the plus sign drawn on the bottom marked North, South, East, and West.

"Now we need to follow her dotted line to the next point, the lion. She didn't mark the distance, so we don't know how far it is. However, the marsh and river are beyond it." He pointed to the left side of the map. "We get to those and we've gone too far. I was listening for the river."

Garrison opened and closed his mouth three times. He knew his eyes were wide, taking in Tuck as though for the first time. He noted the ease with which he carried the satchel and considered the sandwiches it contained earlier. "Have you done this before?"

"What? Follow a map? Of course. Haven't you?"

"Not like this. I mean, sure, one with nice graphics in a video game. I've never actually used one in real life. In the middle of the woods. How do you even know where we are without the blue dot?"

"I'm not sure what you mean by blue dot, but that's not important right now. Using a map means finding landmarks you can reference in the terrain."

"Like the river?"

"Exactly. Now, come on. I do not want to be here when night falls."

They kept walking. Garrison took the little acorn man from his pocket and rolled it around in his fingers. He thought about Carly, about finding the ring. It wouldn't save her, but he vowed that would be his next step.

"Darn it," said Tuck.

"What?"

"That's the start of the marsh. See the bulrushes?"

Garrison looked where Tuck pointed and saw tall green reeds with brown cattails. Were those bulrushes?

"We've gone too far," Tuck spat. "I knew it." He took out the map and glared at it.

Garrison didn't have any help to offer. He knew nothing about maps or hiking. So he adjusted the small metal arm of the acorn man until it was giving him a thumbs up.

"Where did you get the fumsup?"

Garrison noticed Tuck looking at him. "The what?"

Tuck nodded toward Garrison's hand. "The little doll."

"It's not a doll. It's an action figure."

Tuck rolled his eyes.

"Carly made it for me."

"Ooohhh."

"Shut up."

"Can I see it?"

Garrison's stomach did a mini flip. No, he wanted to shout. Instead, he forced himself to hold out the little man for Tuck to take.

Tuck turned it over in his hand.

Garrison pushed his lips together to stop from asking for it back.

"My great grandfather loved Fumsups," Tuck said softly. "He collected them. Used to tell me the history of each one when I was little."

Garrison widened his eyes. This was the first time Tuck spoke about his family.

"Could be because of my family's talent. Since it's related to luck, we have an affinity with objects like fumsups." Tuck handed back the acorn man. "It's a good one. She has talent. Give it a rub."

Garrison felt stupid. He looked at it. The brown acorn shell was dull brown. Was he supposed to rub that? Or the wire thumb? The black dot eyes and pointy nose seemed to mock his wondering. He knew his face was turning red, but he rubbed the head with his index finger.

Nothing happened.

Feeling even redder, he put the acorn man back in his pocket. Something made him look back the way they came. "I think we need to go that way," he said, looking a bit to the left.

"And why is that?" Tuck asked.

Garrison turned back to see him smiling a strange sort of smile. "I don't know. We don't have to."

Tuck shook his head. After adjusting his satchel strap, Tuck said loudly, "Lead on."

Garrison tried to find a path, like Tuck had, but there wasn't one in the direction he wanted to go. They just did the best they could to step over small plants and go around larger ones. Garrison was pretty scratched up by the time he came to an old tree that was as wide across as he was. What made him pause at this particular tree was the bulbous growth on the trunk, a strange bumpy mole that looked heavy enough to pull the tree over.

Garrison squinted at it. "Does that look like a lion?"

Tuck came up beside him, pulling spiny burrs from his shirt. "No."

They walked closer to the tree. "Yeah. Here is the mane," said Garrison, pointing to the way the bark seemed to expand from a central point. "His mouth is open, like he's roaring. We found it!" Garrison hooted and punched the air.

"Calm down, Robinson Crusoe. We still have two more clues." Tuck took out the map. "Now to the pine trees."

"There," said Garrison, pointing over Tuck's shoulder.

"West," said Tuck, folding the map back up. He squinted at the sky. "From where the sun is, I'd say west is that way."

"Let's do it," Garrison said, grinning widely. He felt like a treasure hunter.

They walked until they came to three majestic-looking pines planted in a meandering line. The pines were so large, Garrison couldn't see the upper branches. He wondered how tall they were when his mother put them on her map.

"Are the trees dancing, or are we supposed to dance between them?" Garrison asked.

"Maybe both."

After weaving through the trees, they stopped. "How old was your mother when she made this?" Tuck asked.

Garrison shrugged. "I don't know, 14 or so. She said about my age. Why?"

"Her steps," Tuck said. "She wants us to take seven paces, but that's different for everyone. We should go by yours, but maybe shorten it a bit."

Garrison just stood there, staring.

"What are you waiting for?" Tuck asked.

"For you to say something that makes sense. A pace?"

"Just walk in that direction. But take slightly smaller steps."

"Okay."

Garrison walked, and Tuck counted. "One...two—" Tuck cut off abruptly.

Confused, Garrison turned to him. Tuck put his finger to his lip and pointed.

Garrison turned back and stared. It was not pleasant. When he concentrated on something, the nausea from the double image was worse. He swallowed hard and thought he saw something move. Tuck whispered in his ear. "There's a guard by a downed tree. I think that's where the hiding place is."

Garrison nodded, then slapped his hand over his mouth to keep from vomiting. Maybe he should ask Mae for some of that candied ginger.

"I'll go around to the left, draw the guard away. You head towards that tree. Got it?"

Garrison remembered not to nod and instead muttered a sound similar to yes.

"Shhh," Tuck reprimanded.

Garrison rolled his eyes. It was barely a noise. Tuck was the one doing all the talking.

Tuck put down his bag and turned to the left. He stepped carefully, heel first with each foot. Garrison was astonished at how little noise he made, even going through the brush. He tried to look at the guard again. The person was probably 20 feet away from him, maybe a little less. Garrison took deep breaths through his mouth to quell the nausea and squinted. The figure was large, stocky, mostly likely a he, and resembled a Viking. Brown leather was draped around his body and something appeared to be hanging from his belt. He scanned the area. Had he heard them, Garrison wondered, squatting as low as possible.

A loud pop happened to the left, followed by a sizzle of sparks. It sounded like a firework.

The guard turned and ran in that direction.

Garrison marveled at the guard's stupidity. That was obviously a distraction. Still, it played in their favor. Garrison stood and slowly advanced to the fallen tree. It was lying at an angle away from him, so Garrison could see its long trunk and rib like branches. It was long dead, with mushrooms and moss growing on it. In the village, there must be a field here, because the double image was of crops in neat rows. Garrison tried to ignore it. Mae said he just needed to concentrate. He tried. He looked at the bark of the tree, at the bright white mushroom growing in a branch hollow.

He staggered, but kept staring. The tree seemed to solidify just a fraction. It was enough. Garrison walked towards it, glancing around once for the guard. Nothing. There were some sounds of crunching leaves off in the distance. It made his heart kick up a level.

Other than the mushrooms, there seemed to be nothing remarkable about the tree. Except the bottom. The root ball was pulled from the ground, but still intact. It was massive, easily 5 feet high and 6 across. The roots hung down in tangles like giant dreadlocks.

He went closer and touched one of the roots. It was cool and thick. It felt like part rope and part stem. Very strange.

Then he noticed a shadow below the roots. He pushed a few aside, blinking as clogs of dirt fell toward him. When he opened his eyes, he was staring at a hole. It actually looked more like a crater. He marveled at the size and realized it must be where the roots were in the ground. When the tree fell, the roots tore from the ground, leaving behind this empty space. It never filled up because the roots were covering it. He smiled. This was exactly the type of place where he would hide treasure. It was perfect.

He pushed the roots further aside and climbed in. Dirt fell down the back of his shirt and he jerked around, trying to get it out. There was a bit of water at the very bottom of the hole and the dirt was soft. The temperature was cooler too. Really, if there wasn't the danger of being caught, it would be a cool place to hang out.

He looked around, trying to see in the shadowy light filtering in through the roots. The sides were mostly smooth, as though someone packed them down. In one spot, he almost thought he saw a handprint. He held his hand up to it — a bit bigger, perhaps, but close. He made a 360, looking for anything special. There was a column of small shelves carved into one wall. They were shallow, just deep enough to hold small objects. He crouched down to look. He found a large feather, probably from a hawk, along with many smaller ones. There were also some chunks of white quartz, a perfectly round pebble, a couple of unusual pine cones, a bent nail, a squashed cylinder of rusty metal, and some paper that was illegible. Finally, in the center of the lowest shelf, he saw it. A ring. It was gold with something embossed on the top. Black gunk obscured the design, and Garrison began trying to rub it off on his pants.

Tuck came running.

"I found it," Garrison whispered, peering over the edge of the hole.

Tuck didn't glance at him, but ran to a nearby pine tree and dropped a small pile of rocks. Garrison was glad he wouldn't be at the receiving end of those. "Great. Put it on," said Tuck.

Garrison did. It fit surprisingly well on his index finger. "Done. So now what? Do I call out for the copy? Is there, like, a special whistle?"

"Don't be ridiculous. What do you see?"

"What do you mean, 'what do I see?'"

Tuck rolled his eyes. "When you look around. What do you see?"

Garrison looked. He saw trees, then fields, houses, then bushes. "I see what I always see."

"No! That can't be."

"Why can't it be?"

"Because that means the ring...the power...it went with the copy?"

"Tuck. What are you talking about?"

Tuck didn't answer. He was staring at something. Garrison turned around. Two men were standing there, like they stepped out of thin air.

"Ah, sh—" Tuck started, but one of the men hit him with a club. The other grinned at Garrison, who felt trapped in the hole. He turned to escape out the far side, when he saw another two men standing there.

"Hey, Hog," one yelled to the left. "You can stop flailing about. We got them."

The noise made by the guard Tuck lured away immediately stopped. Then Garrison realized it was a decoy, a distraction. How stupid was he?

He glared at the four men who stood there as the guard joined them. He was the biggest and leered at Garrison. "Come on now, little hero. Our boss wants to see you."

Garrison tried to shake off the large hands that reached in to pull him up, but they held firm. Up he came, like a doll, and was put on the ground. Hog didn't let go.

Tuck still lay on the ground, motionless. Garrison's gut twisted. He's not dead, Garrison told himself. Just unconscious. Not dead. Someone pulled Garrison's hands forward and suddenly gasped.

"Silver!" the man spat. He pushed roughly at Garrison's sleeve, revealing the vambrace.

Hog laughed. "You've got to be kidding."

Garrison felt his face flush. He knew how stupid it looked; the cutlery tied to his arm.

The man in front of him took a knife out of a small sheath on his belt. Garrison stiffened, expecting the worst. The man sliced neatly through the string holding the vambrace. The whole thing fell to the ground in a useless lump. It felt like it took Garrison's hope with it. He hung his head as his hands were tied together. He didn't even resist as he was pushed forward along a path.

Garrison did glance back once for Tuck. Hog had him, fireman style, draped over his broad shoulders. Tuck still didn't move.

Hog pushed his way to the front, leading the rest down a small, rough trail. The dual landscape made everything worse for Garrison. So he stared downward. The path seemed to exist in both worlds, or maybe dirt was dirt. The double image didn't matter.

He was so focused on the ground; he didn't realize they entered a camp until he heard voices calling out. As he looked up, he reeled from the diplopia. Blinking furiously, he tried to focus on one or the other of the two images before him. Ignoring the ghost of trees, he saw a dozen small tents set up in a loose circle. They were tan canvas, each with a fire pit in front. Some of the pits were smoking, topped with large black tripods holding pots or kettles. It would have been a pleasant little camp scene if the men weren't all scowling at him.

Hog was tying Tuck to a tree near the edge of the camp. Garrison could see him struggling against the ropes. That meant Tuck was awake! Garrison couldn't help but smile even as he was shoved roughly in the back. He was forced over to a post in the center of the ring of tents. The rope binding his hands was tied to it, and then the men left. All but one.

Garrison tried to shout over to Tuck, but the man hit him on the shoulder. So Garrison just sat there, staring at the men moving around the camp. Where was Devose? He had to be here. And Carly. Garrison gulped. He didn't see any sign of her either.

As the sun set, the men around the camp gathered close. They glanced at Garrison, then quickly away, talking in low murmurs to each other. Their tone was excited. Something was about to happen. Garrison could feel it.

The air began to vibrate with an invisible current. That's when someone emerged from the dark space between two tents. Garrison knew who it was immediately — the way he stood tall, the arrogant presence. Devose! He was dressed the same as the other night, in a black suit — tailored jacket and with crisp pant legs. His dress shoes were so shiny they reflected the fading light. However, unlike before, his head wasn't that of a stag. It was human.

Something inside Garrison cried out in pain. Carly! Was that why he wanted her blood? To turn himself human? Was Carly still alive, or did this monster take all of it? Garrison glared at Devose, sadness and anger, a hurricane inside him. Devose turned to him and smiled. That's when Garrison realized he had something dark on his head. A crown? No, a set of deer antlers. Devose wasn't completely human after all. Hope about Carly bubbled up, spreading through him.

Devose spoke. "I have been dreaming of this for centuries," he said, then lowered his head, as though to skewer Garrison on the tip of his forked antlers.

Garrison could barely question this move when everything in him suddenly went tight. His lungs sucked in air, fast and shallow, his arm and leg muscles drew taut, ready to spring. He didn't understand what was happening. His body was out of his control. His mind finally caught up with his body — PANIC. That's what he felt. There was an overwhelming need to run away, to hide. He pulled against the ropes binding him.

Then Devose lifted his head.

And Garrison sagged. The tightness in his chest gone, his muscles spent. "What was that?"

Devose began to prowl. "That, human," he spat the word, "is my power. To loose your most primal instincts — the ones that manifest when your survival is threatened. I believe your people named it fight or flight." He made a dismissive gesture. "Ridiculous name. It's fear so engrossing, it can control mobs, overturn rulers and create chaos." Devose clapped his hands like a giddy madman.

"It's just fear?" Garrison asked.

"Just fear?" Devose repeated. Then he laughed. "Fear and anxiety drive you small-minded creatures — you humans. It's what makes me a God among you."

"You're not a God," Garrison said.

Devose narrowed his eyes at him, but continued to move. "How would you know? Have you ever seen a God? Met one? No. Because you're an ignorant. Little. Boy." Devose changed direction, his polished loafer crunching something as he turned. "Just like your grandfather."

"My grandfather?"

"Mmm. He married Mae, and she became keeper of the Wagon Wheel portal. It seemed a beautiful picture, but secretly, Lawrence was jealous. He couldn't see us. And Mae could. He wanted the power for himself."

Garrison shook his head. It couldn't be true.

"He lived in that house for many years and knew where all the belongings from previous owners of the house were stored. He was curious, wondered if another Fotismeno ever owned the house. If there was a way he could become one."

Devose turned and pushed into Garrison's face. "It was so easy to nudge him. For some of my compatriots to fuel his secret desire. When he found the ring," Devose held out his hand, showing Garrison the gold ring. "He kept it a secret. He came out into the forest, where Mae told him there was a village. And he put it on." Devose closed his fist; the knuckle above the ring turned white. "Then we had him."

"I don't understand."

"The ring isn't just a ring. It tears a hole in the fabric between worlds. Lawrence was thrust into ours. He could suddenly see us. And we could touch him. Hurt him. So we did." Devose laughed at the memory.

"No," Garrison muttered.

"Yes. Eventually, he broke free of us. Ran. And we followed. He tried taking the ring off, throwing it away, but it was too late. We went through the tear into the human realm. We pushed on his mind, breaking him."

"So, you killed him?"

Devose stood up straight. "No. He isn't dead. There was no need. You see, when a group of us focuses our talents on a single person, the emotions take over. Fear, shame, rage, guilt — all of it is released at once. It's too much for you fragile humans. The mind SNAPS!" Devose crunched a twig at the same moment, making Garrison flinch. Devose snickered. "Raving like a madman miles from here, he was picked up by some good samaritan who took him to the city. He's in a psych ward there. Crazy."

Garrison could barely breathe. "That's...that's horrible."

"It's merely the natural order."

Garrison looked down. He noticed the ring on his left hand. It was dirtier than Devose's, but it was the same one. "So, it was this ring?"

"Yes. And no," Devose answered. He came forward and produced a sharp knife.

Garrison gasped.

"Music to my ears," Devose muttered, but he concentrated on Garrison's bindings and sliced through the rope. Garrison was free, except for the menacing men forming a wall around them.

Replacing the knife, Devose took Garrison's left hand and stretched the fingers outward. Then he held his left so the tips of their fingers nearly touched. Garrison felt his ring begin to wiggle, then move. Devose's was doing the same. Devose moved away, and the rings flew towards each other in the space between their hands. There was a small explosion of light and Garrison blinked. Floating there in the air between them was a single gold ring, a fusion of the copy and the original. It glowed slightly.

Devose took hold of the ring and Garrison felt heavy with failure. "But how did you even find it? The ring, I mean. I know my mom's map led you to it, but if Lawrence threw it into the woods, how did she get it?"

Devose didn't remove his eyes from the ring when he answered. "I was vexed by that as well. While we poisoned the town against Mae, feeding their suspicion and fear that she killed her husband, I searched in your world every night for the ring. As did my minions. None of us were ever successful. It seems your mother happened upon it while she roamed the forest during a juvenile game. What are the odds? Then she hid it, stuck it in a dirt hole like it was a piece of trash. Ignoramus." Devose pushed at a section of the ring's top, and part of the design moved. Garrison couldn't see properly in the dim light, but it looked like Devose turned something on the ring face and the color around the ring shifted slightly, from a gold to a purple. Then Devose did something unexpected. He slid the ring back onto Garrison's finger.

"What are you doing?" Garrison asked.

"Helping you to see."

The minute Devose let go, the world around Garrison shifted. It was like a movie where one image smoothly melts into another. The double image of trees and brush slid away, revealing the tents, small fires and a distant village. There were farm fields all around them, sprinkled with rows of old trees. He saw them all before, but now it was like an optometrist dropped the correct lens into the eye machine and everything was bright and clear. "Your world?" Garrison found himself asking.

"Yes."

"How?"

"The ring is ancient. The power fused within it can do many things. For both of us."

"But why give it back to me?"

"Because," Devose said, his lips a slash across his face. "After we kill you in our world, I will take it. No copy. No original. Just one ring from now until eternity. Your friend over there knows."

Garrison looked in Tuck's direction, torn between horror and curiosity.

Devose raised his voice a little so it would carry to Tuck. "I knew your family eons ago. Smugglers, black market traders. WONDERFUL people." Devose said it with a smile.

Tuck raised his head a little. Garrison sucked in air.

"I was counting on the fact that you would figure it out. That you would understand about copying human objects. And it appears you did. No doubt believing its power, in the hands of a true Fotismeno, would repel me. What a charming notion. But this particular object is cloaked in secrets. You never had a chance. Instead, you brought me exactly what I needed — a Fotismeno crossing over, wearing the ring. So that death can lock it in place."

Garrison saw Tuck's chest lift sharply, as though he took a quick breath. It was far too dark to see his eyes, but Garrison knew Tuck must be looking at him. Was Tuck gripped by the same word suddenly echoing in his mind? Death!

Devose continued in a voice bright with amusement. "I can see from the young Fotismeno's expression, you didn't mention that part. How exceptionally tantalizing." Devose paused. "Although, in truth, I hoped it would be Mae who came, not the boy. Pity. But no matter." He turned to the men around him. "It's time, gentlemen." Then he lowered his head once again. They all did.

Garrison sucked in a breath, anticipating the fear, the tightness. It came again, strong, but there was more too. So much more.

His father's voice in his head — an overheard conversation. "Rachel, I refuse to stay here and watch you give into his weirdness! I want a divorce." Garrison's stomach was suddenly on fire.

His mom's face when she was forced to ask his father for money because Garrison needed clothes, or shoes, or wanted guitar lessons. The way she fake laughed when she called to pick up extra shifts because his birthday was coming up. Each memory was a stone weighing him down. He fell to his knees.

A woman's voice was telling him to "GET OUT," he wasn't welcome. Angry glares from strangers. Evilly grinning boys coming at him with fists. Garrison could almost feel their malice like physical blows. Disapproval opened bloody gashes in his psyche. No one wanted him.

Garrison felt his body start to shake. His chest was impossibly tight, like it was caged by zip ties. A sound came from his lips. A sob maybe. He couldn't hold these emotions, the guilt, the shame, the loneliness. He collapsed. The pressure inside was too much. He needed it to stop. He took a deep breath, but instead of air, he inhaled dirt.

That was the moment something inside him changed.

At once, all his focus went to his throat, the way the dirt stuck to the back of it and made his esophagus convulse. The way his lungs screamed for air. The physical sensations opened a tiny space in his mind. A space that looked at his distress and thought, "What's happening? These are inside your head. No one is touching you. You're doing this to yourself!"

Devose took a step closer to him. "You should have stayed away, Fotismeno," he growled. "I didn't know you had power until you arrived. Now, I'll use you to end Mae's line, the protection of the Wagon Wheel farm, everything."

Garrison couldn't help but picture it — the large white house as wreckage with Mae lying pale and motionless on the ground. Tuck, Rebecca, Sam, Carly — all gone. Him alone. Again.

He ground his teeth against the black hole of pain reopening inside him. The dirt in his mouth crunched between his molars, leaving a metallic tang on his tongue. It helped. He focused on that. On how the ground felt cold on his exposed skin. How he could smell smoke.

Just like when Tuck burned trash. Garrison pictured Tuck's face standing near the firepit, telling the story of another prank. Suggesting more. He imagined Hilde, how her fur felt when he nuzzled her. It tickled his nose. His fingers twitched as he thought about sliding them through it. Then Carly petting her, smiling.

Carly!

His breath stuttered. The space Garrison formed, separating him from the shattering emotions, closed fast. His anxiety over Carly's possible fate was an oil spill in the ocean of his clearing mind. It threatened to cover everything in thick, sticky darkness.

In desperation, Garrison remembered Mae's note to him the first morning in the attic. The last line. The words she scribbled out. He was almost sure she wrote, I love you.

The squeezing stopped. He thought of her smile over a mug of coffee. The way her eyes twinkled sometimes when she looked at him during dinner.

Garrison's heart began to beat warm in his chest. He felt joy, and with each beat, the tightness eased. He closed his eyes, remembering eating popsicles on hot summer days, scrubbing icing off cabinets, Carly's smile, Hilde's purr. There was enough room in his head now to realize the effects of Devose were lessening. He pushed himself up, first to his knees, then to his legs. When he was standing again, Garrison opened his eyes.

Everyone around him gasped. "His eyes," they yelled at each other. "Look at his eyes. I've seen none that bright before."

Garrison stared at each person individually, and then at Devose.

Devose was still bent, antlers to Garrison's chest. "Give me back the ring," he demanded through clenched teeth.

Garrison barely heard it. He felt 10 feet tall, a giant towering above the scene with Devose. His mind continued to feed him images — Tuck saving him from the gang of boys, of Rebecca fussing over his eating, of Sam telling him he was special.

Devose took a step backwards. "It seems I misjudged you."

Garrison wanted to laugh. That was the story of his life. But he knew that if he gave in now, it would diminish whatever was happening to him. He pushed the self-doubt away. Without knowing why, he lifted the ring to his face. Around the central design was a small circle of scrollwork. Except that Garrison knew suddenly that it wasn't scrollwork. It was an inscription, written in a language

Garrison never saw before, yet knew deep down how to speak.

Skoteinó pros fos.
Fóvos sti gnósi.
Cháos deméno
Cháos deméno
Cháos deméno

Devose's leg spasmed, knocking him off balance. It shot forward, the pant leg tearing open as bulky muscle shot out. It was covered in dull gray, brown fur.

"No," Devose screamed, gripping it. His loafer shot off as his foot shrank and hardened into a deer hoof. "Help me," he yelled. Yet there was no one to help him. The men in the camp were running away, yelling at their companions.

Garrison advanced on Devose. Repeating the words.

"Garrison?"

The voice broke through Garrison's concentration. It was Carly. She was still alive! She was standing in between tents. He ran towards her, not stopping until his arms were around her in a bear hug. She squeezed him back.

"I thought I'd never see you again," he whispered.

She sobbed in his ear.

He pushed her away from him to examine her. That's when he saw the wrapping on her wrist, the faintest rust-colored stain evidence of her blood. He whirled around to face Devose, shielding Carly from view. But Devose was gone. Movement near the far edge of the camp caught his eye. A tall man limping as he tried to run with the leg of a deer.

"He's gone," said Tuck from the tree. "Maybe, I don't know, you could untie me now?"

Garrison walked over to him, still scanning the camp for danger. He tried to untie the rope, but it was too tight. Carly found a knife in a tent and cut Tuck free. As soon as he was up and standing, he glared at Carly. "Why did you do it?"

Carly backed up. "Do what?"

"Call out to Garrison. You distracted him. Let Devose get away."

"I...I..." Carly's body shook. Her eyes were wide as she leaned away from him.

Tuck's voice was venom. "Whose side are you on?"

Garrison stepped towards them. "Tuck, chill. Give her a second to explain." They both turned to him, and he nodded at Carly, encouraging her.

"I didn't realize what you were doing," she said. "I heard a bunch of yelling and then my guard left. So I ran. I was sneaking through the tents and saw you, Garrison." She pointed to the spot where she had been while he faced Devose. "From there, I couldn't even see Devose. Just you. And you were practically glowing. I just called out in surprise. I didn't mean for Devose to get away."

Garrison saw Tuck look at the spot between the two tens and work out the angles in his head. Her view of Devose would have been blocked. Tuck nodded, his shoulders and back noticeably more relaxed.

Garrison relaxed too. The power inside him, what made him glow, was ebbing. He felt shaky and tired. "What do we do now?"

Tuck smiled. "We go home."

"Great."

They started walking. Garrison picked up a long stick to lean on. He stopped when he noticed Carly wasn't with them. She was standing alone a few yards behind them, head hanging. He looked at Tuck, who rolled his eyes.

"Fine," he said quietly. Then he spoke louder. "Aren't you coming?"

Carly looked up. "But...I thought...well..."

"It'll be alright," said Garrison. "Come on."

Carly smiled a little and came towards them.

Tuck turned forward. "This way," he said, leading them back along the path.

Garrison let Carly fall into the step next to him. She eyed the ring still on his hand, but didn't say anything about it. And neither did he.

CHAPTER 32

Around the table, everyone stared at Garrison. He just finished telling them all what had happened. He looked at each of them to see what they were thinking.

Mae was straight-faced.

Sam had deep furrows between his eyebrows.

Rebecca's lip was quivering.

Tuck's eyes roamed over everyone's faces.

Carly was looking at her lap. Garrison's heart went out to her. He wanted her to be able to stay, but it wasn't his decision. He hoped what Mae read in the journal would be enough. And that Carly gave herself up to stall Devose.

Finally, Mae spoke. "Sam, is it possible?"

Garrison wasn't sure which part of the story she was referring to.

"In theory?" Sam rubbed his beard and shrugged at the same time.

Mae looked Garrison in the eyes. "I'm really not sure what to do. I'm fighting my impulse to barricade you in the attic. You've proved you can take care of yourself, I suppose. I had no idea there was a way to transform him. You say it's on the ring?"

Garrison nodded, sliding the ring from his finger and handing it to her. She stared at it. Garrison pictured it in his mind. The top half of the small circular face was a sun rising from the horizon. Rays were arranged around it like a star. At the center of the sun was an eye, because there's always an eye on creepy relics. Below the horizon, the background was enameled black with a small raised image that might be part of a rope. Garrison wished he could show it to his eighth grade English teacher who loved poetry and symbolism. They did an entire unit on interpreting your dreams. He was sure Miss Wanschmidt would understand what it meant.

Apparently, Mae wasn't an English teacher. She shook her head and held it out to Sam. He took it.

"I don't recognize the design, although something is familiar. The symbols around the edge, those look Greek. I will need a bit of time to translate it."

"Why don't we just use Google Translate?" Garrison asked. He ran to his room for his cell phone. Luckily, it still had some battery life left since he wasn't using it. He raced back to the dining room. "Okay, how do I get on your internet?" He was speaking to Mae, although he was looking at the phone. There were still no Wi-Fi networks.

"I use a hot spot."

Garrison wanted to slap himself. Why didn't he think to try that? He went into settings and searched. Only one came up — a random string of numbers and letters. "What's the password?" he asked.

Mae took a bit too long to answer, making Garrison look up. She looked away. "Rachel," she said. "Capital R and the L is a number one."

A warm ball slid into Garrison's stomach as he typed in his mother's name. He opened Google Translate and held out his hand for the ring. Sam gave it to him, and Garrison positioned his phone over the main design. "Okay. It keeps shifting, but I think it says, Dark to light. Fear to knowledge. Chaos bound. Chaos bound. Chaos bound."

"Let's hope that means it's bonding chaos and not the alternative," Sam muttered. He was rubbing the back of Rebecca's shoulders, comforting her.

"But if it was Greek, how did I know how to speak it?" Garrison asked.

Sam shook his head.

"Blood," Carly interjected. "You are a Fotismeno, a descendant of those who originally trapped him. The powers you have, the special abilities, it connects you to all those that came before. You're a bit like me. When I first learned to shift, it was like I knew how to do it. My muscles knew, my mind knew. My mother told me it was because of my ancestors. A kin to a muscle memory from lifetimes before yours, all passed down through blood, bone and sinew. That's how you knew." She nodded for emphasis.

Garrison didn't know what to say to that. He had a bunch of dead ancestors inside him? He held the ring out to Mae, but she shook her head.

"But it's yours?"

She pushed her lips together, making a thin line. "I don't think it is."

Garrison inspected the ring, thinking about that. He slid it back on his finger. It felt heavier now.

Finally, Mae turned to Carly. "Why didn't you tell us you were a shapeshifter?"

Sam spoke before Carly could answer. "Honestly, it makes sense she wouldn't, Mae. You would understand. If you lived through the shapeshifter purge." He shook his head. "Dozens of shifters rounded up and tortured to find others. A wildfire of distrust and fear that spread across our world. Many people died, wrongly. There were atrocities, even by the royal families, that can never be forgiven." Sam looked down, a shadow over his face. Pain, Garrison decided. And possibly guilt.

Rebecca put her hand on his, and it broke the spell. The shadow was gone. Sam's eyes were still sad, but he smiled at her and patted her hand.

Carly cleared her throat. "I have a question," she said, looking at Rebecca. She swallowed audibly. "Devose took my blood and drank it to become more human." She held up her wrist with the bandage. "Then I couldn't shift. Is it gone forever?"

"From the little I know of shapeshifters," said Rebecca, "their power can't be transferred or lost. Not like that. I would wager he just took so much; you were too weak. Were you quite sleepy?"

"Yes!" Garrison could see the relief on Carly's face. It was like someone turned on a lightbulb inside her.

"I would predict that as your body replaces the lost blood, you'll regain your power."

There was silence again. Garrison looked at Carly, but she stayed silent. He decided he would ask. "She needs a place to recover. Well, live, really."

Mae spoke up before he finished. "Well, it's a good thing this old farmhouse has so many rooms, then."

"Really?" asked Carly, biting her bottom lip. Garrison squinted at the bright glow of her face.

Mae glanced at her, then looked down into her coffee mug. She cleared her throat. "Of course. Think nothing of it."

"We should probably keep her ability a secret from visitors," said Rebecca. "If and when the Wagon Wheel reopens."

Sam nodded emphatically.

"Agreed," Mae said. She looked at Tuck and Garrison.

"Absolutely," Garrison said immediately, crossing his heart. Then he realized this was stupid. No one besides Mae probably even knew what the gesture meant.

"Tuck?" Mae asked when he didn't reply.

Tuck's expression was strange. "I'm not against you," he dragged out the words, "but my sentence...part of it is a vow of fidelity. I'm not sure...I just can't promise. But I will do my very best to evade revealing your secret." He looked at Carly and patted his chest near his heart twice with his index finger. Garrison thought it looked a lot like crossing your heart. He made a mental note for the future.

Everyone went quiet again, lost in their own thoughts. Then Rebecca turned to Mae and asked, "What are you going to do about...about Lawrence?"

Mae scrubbed her face with her hand. "I don't know."

"But he's alive. He didn't even leave you. It wasn't you at all."

"I wouldn't say that. Sounds like he was jealous."

"This would clear your name, Mae," Sam suggested.

Mae began massaging her forehead with both hands, like it was painful. "It's just...he left. Died. I accepted all that. But now, I know he didn't. Maybe. Can we even believe Devose? And if we do, it means Lawrence found the ring and kept it a secret from me. A secret that let Devose come into our home decades later and nearly destroy it. How can I just get over that?"

Rebecca leaned forward. "You should go see him, at least."

Mae stood up fast. Her chair tipped backwards just enough to slam down against the floor and rock slightly. "I can't...I just can't even think about this now." She left the dining room.

They all looked at each other. "I'll go talk to her," Sam said. He gave Rebecca a kiss on the top of her head and departed. Rebecca excused herself, leaving Garrison, Tuck, and Carly alone at the table.

"What do you think Devose will do next?" Garrison asked. "Try to come after Carly's blood again?"

Tuck shrugged. "I'm not sure. It depends if the men he convinced to follow him are more afraid of you than him."

"Afraid of me?"

"Yea. Mister all powerful Fotismeno." Tuck snickered.

Garrison punched him in the shoulder. Lightly.

Carly looked thoughtful. "I could ask. I know people close to Devose. You know, from living at his house." She didn't meet either of their eyes.

"Might be useful," said Tuck.

"As long as it's safe," said Garrison.

Carly nodded. She stood up. "I'll go do it now." She headed into the hall.

"Where do you think she's going?" Garrison asked.

Tuck rolled his eyes. "Lovesick looks disgusting on you."

"Shut up. Seriously, where? To her old room?"

"That would be my guess."

"But she can have any of the rooms. That one is so tiny."

"Sometimes we like things that are familiar. Speaking of rooms, let's go see if ours survived Mae's safeguarding."

Garrison groaned. "What a shame if it didn't."

CHAPTER 33

A week later, Carly raced back to her room from the mailbox, a letter clutched to her chest. Since she wrote to Sune, she had checked every day for his reply. Finally, here it was. She recognized the loopy way he wrote her name.

Once inside her room, she locked the door. She still loved the feeling of being able to lock her own door, and unlock it, when she wished.

She sat on her bed and flipped over the envelope. Her fingers shook as she tore open the top. A blank piece of paper was inside. But she knew better. She used her finger to rub hard on the center. The friction of her fingers created heat, revealing the hidden message.

Dear Carly,

I was surprised, but pleased to get your letter. I'm glad you remembered the invisible ink. My dad is home now and he's furious. He knows someone helped you escape and suspects everyone. Except me. He still considers me muddle-brained and unable to form even simple thoughts — his words. The usual.

From what I've overheard, things are not going well for him. A contingent of the queen's army was still near the village when the Fotismeno appeared. Devose's men ran straight into them. Most are locked up for treason now. Any that escaped are in hiding. The Coalition of the Stag is over.

I don't think my dad plans to go after you. He's made no mention of it. In fact, I think he's wallowing in self-pity. Such weakness. I'll let you know if things change. Keep writing. I have mail duty, so there's little danger of being discovered, but I burned your letter after reading it, anyway. I suggest you do the same to mine.

I miss you, Carly.

Yours always,

Sune

Carly leaned back against her bed's pillows. Devose was home. That meant he was back in Perlscrest, hundreds of miles away, and his precious army was gone. They won! She smiled to herself. She would tell Tuck, so he could take the news to the queen. But first...she got up. There was no fireplace in her room, so she went to the bathroom, tore the letter into tiny pieces and threw them into the toilet. The ink faded as it absorbed the water. Then she flushed.

She decided not to tell Tuck who Sune was, that he was the heir to the throne of darkness and Devose's son. Instead, she would encourage him, and everyone, to assume Sune was just a boy who worked at the estate. They didn't need to know the truth. More than likely, they wouldn't understand, branding him a double agent who would betray her. She toyed with that idea for a moment; Sune luring her back into Devose's clutches. Then she shook her head. He was her closest friend, rescued her once, and even risked himself by writing to her. She could trust him.

CHAPTER 34

It was a blazing day in August, two months after Garrison arrived at the Wagon Wheel farm. The sun was golden in the sky and the slightly faded blades of grass swayed gently in the breeze. The house and porch were teeming with members of the Anthropi Avra, the portal having been reopened by the queen. Many of the visitors wanted an unofficial look at the new Fotismeno, driving Garrison, Tuck, and Carly away. They escaped many days into the woods, a place Mae now let them explore freely, even if reluctantly. One of their favorite places to go was the fallen tree his mom found as a girl. True, it was where they got captured, but the place didn't feel threatening. It felt...comfortable.

They were sitting on the dead tree trunk, picking at mushrooms, when a semi-familiar noise floated in the air towards them. A car engine. Not just driving down the road, but getting closer, closer, then stopping.

"Sounds like your ride's here," said Tuck.

Garrison stood. He couldn't see anything through the trees, but at this point, he knew the direction of the house. He started walking. Carly and Tuck followed.

Tiny moths started unfurling in his stomach. Everything was so different now. Would his mom be different? Did he want her to be?

"Does she know about her father?" Carly asked. "That he's still alive?"

Garrison nodded. "Mae emailed her. Said some staff member at the facility found an old missing person's record on him and reached out to her. I guess my mom was shocked."

"Not surprising. But I'm sure she was also thrilled. She'll finally get to meet her dad."

Garrison nodded, but it made him wonder about Carly's father. Did she know who he was? Garrison doubted it and now didn't feel like the right time to ask, not when he was leaving.

When they arrived at the house, Carly and Tuck slowed. Garrison continued on. He could see his mother talking to Mae. "Mom!"

She turned, her brown hair lifting a little in the breeze, like it was in slow motion. She smiled a smile that was just hers. Garrison realized how much he missed her. He ran to her and squeezed.

She squeezed back. "I missed you."

He looked up and there were tears in her eyes.

"Come on now," Mae complained. "None of that. This isn't a time for tears." She had her hands in her pockets and wouldn't make eye contact. "Let's have some coffee and iced tea." She turned to walk into the house.

"Tell me all about your summer," his mother said as they followed, an arm draped over his shoulders. Mae turned back and Garrison met her eyes. Mae shrugged almost imperceptibly.

As they sat at the kitchen island, Garrison cleared his throat. "I learned how to get frosting out of cabinet hinges."

His mother laughed.

He took the glass of iced tea from Mae.

"Wait, you're serious?" asked his mother.

Mae jumped in. "Actually, he was a tremendous help this summer," she said. "With more than just cleaning."

His mother looked between them. She smiled. "It sounds like you two have—"

Sam walked into the kitchen at that moment. "Mae, there's...Oh. I apologize."

"What are you two looking at?" Rachel asked.

"Nothing," Mae said, getting up. "I'll be right back."

Rachel turned to Garrison, her brow furrowed.

"I got a cat," said Garrison, changing the subject. "Let me get her." He ran out into the hall. Sam was showing Mae a letter. She was shaking her head.

"Everything okay?" he asked.

They both looked at him. For a moment, he thought they wouldn't answer.

"The queen summoned Tuck," Mae said.

"Again? Why?"

"She never says."

"He's going to hate that."

Mae nodded. "So we're going to wait to tell him. No sense spoiling your last day here."

Garrison felt those words in his stomach. Relief swirling clockwise. Guilt moving counterclockwise. He took a deep breath, trying to still it.

"Okay?" Mae asked, a bit of the old edge in her voice.

Garrison nodded.

"He'll be back," said Sam, laying a hand on Garrison's shoulder. "He always is."

Garrison smiled slightly, and Mae shooed him away. He ran to his room and grabbed Hilde.

When he returned to the kitchen, his mother said, "I was wondering where you'd got to."

He held Hilde up to her, back legs dangling.

"Aw." His mother extended one finger to pet the cat. "She's lovely, Garrison, but you know I'm..." She sneezed.

"I know, Mom. Mae said she could live here."

"She did? In the house?"

Garrison nodded, pulling Hilde into his chest and rubbing her under the chin. She purred and butted her head against his palm.

His mom made a surprised murmur.

At that moment, Tuck sauntered into the kitchen from outside. He sat on a stool opposite Garrison. Garrison tried not to look at him, but then Tuck started making faces.

"What's so funny?" asked his mother.

"Uh...the cat's whiskers tickle." Garrison put Hilde down on the floor. "I need some more iced tea." He went over to the fridge to avoid looking at Tuck. Luckily, Mae came back into the kitchen then. Garrison was in time to see Mae give Tuck her narrowed-eyed glare and he bolted. Mae went to sit at the island across from his mother. She had her usual coffee.

"So, Mom. Did you decide about going to see him? Lawrence, I mean. My dad. Gosh, that's weird to say."

"I don't know," Mae answered, staring into her mug. "I suppose I should schedule a visit. See if it's really him."

"Do you think there's been a mistake? You said they sent a photo."

"Right. No, I suppose it can't be a mistake."

"Which facility is it again? I don't think you said."

Mae tapped a finger on the ceramic. "Eh. I can't recall at the moment. I've got it somewhere, though."

His mom nodded, like she understood. Personally, Garrison doubted it. Mae was lying. She didn't know which facility or have a photograph. But she refused to tell his mother about Devose and the others, so she made up this story. His mom put a hand on Mae's and said softly, "I can go with you, if you want. If it would make it easier."

Mae almost smiled. And nodded. "Thank you, Rachel. But now, tell us all about your time in Venezuela before you have to go back to the city."

His mother smiled widely and brought out her phone. "There were parrots everywhere. Here, I have a picture."

They talked more about Venezuela and looked at her pictures. Then his mom checked her watch. "Ooh. We better start heading home."

"I'll grab my bag," Garrison said. He scooped Hilde up from the floor and headed to his room. Tuck was inside, lounging on the bed with his guitar. He wondered if Tuck knew about the message from the queen yet. Unlikely. Garrison put Hilde down on the bed next to his suitcase, which he already had packed. "Well, I gotta go," he said in Tuck's general direction.

Tuck stopped strumming. "Yeah."

There was silence.

"Maybe you could visit sometime?"

"Why would I do that?" Tuck said, but Garrison could hear a smile in his voice.

Garrison rolled his eyes. He smiled back. Hilde bumped his hand. "Okay, okay." He picked her up and grabbed the litter box. "You sure you can't take care of her?" Garrison asked.

Tuck's answer was firm. "Positive."

Garrison left the room, shaking his head. He took the main stairs up, climbing two at a time, until he reached the second floor. He went to Carly's door and knocked.

She opened it immediately.

He couldn't help but stare. She was beautiful, long reddish brown hair looping gracefully around her face. She smiled at him, her freckles vivid on her light skin.

His face suddenly felt hot and his shirt collar itched. "Umm. I'm wondering, since I have to go..." he trailed off and held the cat out. "I know you didn't want to before, but I thought maybe now...Tuck doesn't want to and I know how much you love her. Just like I do. If you still don't though, I can ask Mae to—"

"NO!" Carly rushed in to grab Hilde. She stepped so close, Garrison could feel the heat from her body. Her smell, something like minty gum and shampoo, lingered in his nostrils and he had to mentally shake himself to remember what he was saying. "Mae keeps her food in the kitchen, but you'll have to fill her dish. One small scoop a day. She doesn't need the formula anymore. Oh, and check her water. She likes it refilled with fresh every few hours."

Carly made a small noise of agreement and held Hilde up to give her an Eskimo kiss.

Garrison itched his own nose. "And here's her litter box." He put it down next to Carly's dresser. "There's more litter in the downstairs hall. I can bring it up for you, if you want."

Putting the cat on her bed, Carly turned to him. "That's alright. I'll find it." Her emerald eyes glittered. "Thanks, Garrison."

He swallowed. He would miss her terribly, but he couldn't say that. What if she didn't feel the same?

"I'll miss you." The words were no sooner out of her mouth than she stepped forward again and hugged him. It was brief. He barely had time to return it before she pulled away. But when she did, he thought her cheeks looked a little flushed. Was that wishful thinking? He probably looked like a radish. He swallowed hard. "I'll miss you too."

They were silent, eyes meeting, then darting away. Garrison thought he heard his mother call from downstairs. "Well, I better go."

Carly moved back and picked up Hilde again. "Bye," she whispered, nuzzling the light gray fur.

A few minutes later, Garrison's mother was at the car door, having put his suitcase in the trunk. He was on the porch standing before Mae, who was avoiding eye contact.

Garrison went up to her, anyway. "Thanks for having me, Grandma." At the unfamiliar word, she met his gaze. "And everything," Garrison added. "It was really cool."

She started to smile, and he stepped in to hug her.

An instant later, he felt her arms close around him. "You're welcome here anytime, Garrison," she said, her voice quiet.

He let go, nodding, and headed towards the car. This was harder than he expected. Opening his door, he paused to look around the farm. The giant house, solid and safe, if shedding paint like dandruff. There were chickens and cats running around the yard. The air smelled like warm dirt and was alive with insects. He let his gaze travel away to the West, following a dirt road to where it led to a small village. It was the other world.

He looked down at his ring, which he was still wearing. In fact, he never took it off. Now he removed it, having to pull rather hard to pass over his knuckle.

He looked at the ring's face. The eye in the sun had a deep groove around it. Devose did something to that eye, something that changed Garrison's view of the world.

He wedged his fingernail underneath the eye and tried to lift it. It raised up a millimeter, just enough for him to twist it around 180 degrees until it stopped. Then he pressed the eye back in and slid the ring into place on his finger. He looked again at the land beyond the farm. Grass, trees, and cornfields, some stalks already looking a little golden at the edges. The village was gone, although if he tried, he thought he could still detect the smell of chimney smoke.

He heard his mother's door close. He looked at her sitting in the driver's seat of the car.

She looked back at him, her forehead a series of furrows. "You alright?"

He slid into the passenger seat without answering and took one last look at the house. Sam, Rebecca, Tuck and Carly were standing on the tiny side porch now, wedged behind Mae. He waved at them.

His mother turned the key in the ignition. "You'll see her again," she whispered, staring at the porch. Garrison made a vow to himself that he would. He would see all of them again.

ABOUT THE AUTHOR

After 17 years of writing for trade magazines, Emily Refermat jumped full-time into capturing the stories that play in her head. That way others could get to know and love the characters as much as she does. She pens young adult fiction/fantasy, such as her debut magical realism novel *The Invisible War*. When she isn't writing, she's spending quality time with her husband, her three children, and their loveable, if hairy, golden retriever in Southeast Wisconsin.

Note from Emily Refermat

Word-of-mouth is crucial for any author to succeed. If you enjoyed *The Invisible War*, please leave a review online — anywhere you are able. Even if it's just a sentence or two. It would make all the difference and would be very much appreciated.

Thanks!
Emily Refermat

We hope you enjoyed reading this title from:

www.blackrosewriting.com

Subscribe to our mailing list – *The Rosevine* – and receive
FREE books, daily deals, and stay current with news about
upcoming releases and our hottest authors.
Scan the QR code below to sign up.

Already a subscriber? Please accept a sincere thank you for
being a fan of Black Rose Writing authors.

View other Black Rose Writing titles at
www.blackrosewriting.com/books and use promo
code
PRINT to receive a **20% discount** when purchasing.